# KEKA

## THIS CAN HAPPEN TO YOU

PRASAD DESHPANDE

Copyright © Prasad Deshpande
All Rights Reserved.

This book has been self-published with all reasonable efforts taken to make the material error-free by the author. No part of this book shall be used, reproduced in any manner whatsoever without written permission from the author, except in the case of brief quotations embodied in critical articles and reviews.

The Author of this book is solely responsible and liable for its content including but not limited to the views, representations, descriptions, statements, information, opinions and references ["Content"]. The Content of this book shall not constitute or be construed or deemed to reflect the opinion or expression of the Publisher or Editor. Neither the Publisher nor Editor endorse or approve the Content of this book or guarantee the reliability, accuracy or completeness of the Content published herein and do not make any representations or warranties of any kind, express or implied, including but not limited to the implied warranties of merchantability, fitness for a particular purpose. The Publisher and Editor shall not be liable whatsoever for any errors, omissions, whether such errors or omissions result from negligence, accident, or any other cause or claims for loss or damages of any kind, including without limitation, indirect or consequential loss or damage arising out of use, inability to use, or about the reliability, accuracy or sufficiency of the information contained in this book.

Made with ♥ on the Notion Press Platform
www.notionpress.com

# Contents

| | |
|---|---|
| *Foreword* | v |
| 1. Chapter 1 | 1 |
| 2. Chapter 2 | 4 |
| 3. Chapter 3 | 7 |
| 4. Chapter 4 | 11 |
| 5. Chapter 5 | 17 |
| 6. Chapter 6 | 26 |
| 7. Chapter 7 | 33 |
| 8. Chapter 8 | 42 |
| 9. Chapter 9 | 50 |
| 10. Chapter 10 | 69 |
| 11. Chapter 11 | 79 |
| 12. Chapter 12 | 87 |
| 13. Chapter 13 | 95 |
| 14. Chapter 14 | 102 |
| 15. Chapter 15 | 113 |
| 16. Chapter 16 | 120 |
| 17. Chapter 17 | 130 |
| 18. Chapter 18 | 136 |
| 19. Chapter 19 | 149 |
| 20. Chapter 20 | 157 |
| 21. Chapter 21 | 163 |
| 22. Chapter 22 | 171 |
| 23. Chapter 23 | 178 |

# Contents

| | |
|---|---|
| 24. Chapter 24 | 199 |
| 25. Chapter 25 | 208 |
| 26. Chapter 26 | 218 |
| 27. Chapter 27 | 225 |
| Post Word | 231 |

# Foreword

*As usual, the statutory warning...*

**This work is entirely fiction. Any resemblance to anyone, any place or any incidence is purely coincidental - or - maybe, your wild imagination...**

When you travel international - be sure to listen to the tour guide's instructions - or else - you may face massive problems. There are various rules and regulations that govern the travel and are different for different countries around the world.

This story in based in Malaysia and **KEKACAUAN** is a Malay word - meaning Chaos / Mess / Turmoil / Trouble / Shambles / Topsy-Turvy / where everything goes wrong, etc.

The local Malaysian people are good at heart and helpful in nature and I thank them for the hospitality they have shown when I travelled to Malaysia...

They are almost as multilingual and multi-cultured as India and they do have people who speak Tamil and Punjabi. Basically, they are the people who were shifted by British during the colonial rule...

Fasten your seat belt for a whirlwind of a fiction adventure - you will get everything that you need as entertainment from this story... and of course, some tour of Malaysia...

This is a story I wrote in 2010 - about 14 years ago. You may feel the references are a bit out of time... Especially, people have forgotten about the terrorism and the bomb blasts India was accustomed to... 26/11 was fresh in my mind when I wrote this book...

# CHAPTER ONE

It was a bit darkish in the room. He had been waiting impatiently for Col Khanna to reappear.

He had checked every bolt in the room - they were secured - no chance - no hope of escape. The room had interiors of medieval times - the furniture was heavy in weight, made out of strong and thick mahogany - exquisitely carved in oriental style.

The doors were thick and sound proof. The curtains were pulled up for security, from any prying eyes...

He closed his eyes and prayed, "God! Please let her be safe, sound and healthy."

He had nothing more to do than wait for his fate - the way he had been waiting all day long for any news of what the fate had for him...

The door opened creakily and he saw a lean person walk in, "Dinner, Sir..."

That's all he said, kept the tray on the table and walked out - bolting the door behind him...

He was hungry but he couldn't eat. He was worried. Finally, the hunger got better of him and he ate his food quietly - still - no sign of Col Khanna.

He slept a terrible sleep - all that had happened in the past few days came up in tits and bits, in his dreams - it was more of a delirium... Finally, he saw her in his dream - smiling as ever and he slept off...

He woke up in the morning - eager to hear some news - but the entire day passed off in seclusion. This was his fifth day in seclusion - he had been incommunicado since he was brought in - there was no entertainment - no TV - no radio - the SIM card in his mobile had no roaming facility - all he could do was look at the photos in his mobile and smile in her memories - with every smile that appeared on his face - his concern about her safety grew...

He was about to change into his sleeping gear when he heard the door to the room unbolted. He sat upright and alert... "Did you find her?" that was the first question at soon as he saw Col Khanna.

"Yes - we did." came the reply in a very calculated and a solemn voice.

"How is she?"

"I'm sorry - but we found her in a very bad shape - it took us about 5 hours to identify her..."

"Identify?"

"Well, here is the deal..." Col Khanna's voice was curt now, "midnight, we ship you out of here to Subang International Airport amid security and then put you on a chartered flight to New Delhi - I will be glad when I hear the news that you have reached safely."

"Alright - I will go - but before I go..." he pleaded - nay - almost begged, "Can I see her once?"

"No." was the curt answer... "look here son, last 5 days have been hectic for me, trying to save you - if you go out of this place - it will be the way I want - the other option is to get out your way - and face the Judiciary trial - or get killed by those people..."

"Maybe..." he said hopefully, "You can bring her here - I swear - I will not even meet her... and just leave, looking at her without saying a word."

"I wish I could do that son." Col Khanna said musingly," but she is in police custody at a morgue - we found her half eaten away by fish, in complete horrible state..."

"NO!" he cried out in pain as tears overflowed.

He took almost an hour to recover from his pain and shock - to be his normal self. He obeyed Col Khanna's instructions without a murmur...

"I don't say this to anyone..." said Col Khanna, "but as an exception - I will say it to you..." he shook hands, "Thank You - Chaits..."

## CHAPTER TWO

It was raining heavily and he could see nothing out of the window as his plane taxied out to take off - or were the tears in his eyes blinding his vision?

It was almost 5AM in his watch as the plane touched down at Palam airport in Delhi. He soon realized - it was about 3AM - he had not changed the time in his watch according to the IST. He was whisked away through a special clearance channel amid high security. He travelled in a luxurious car but couldn't see anything outside - the windows were blindfolded for security.

He rested for a couple of days amid his seclusion and was then taken to some secret army HQ. He was showered with praises by many officers for the courage he had shown on a foreign land. He then was taken to another cell within...

He was breathless - he was standing face to face - it was the President of India - Dr A.P.J. Abdul Kalam Sir - his joyous wonder knew no bounds when the shower of praises and vote of thanks came right from the President who was his ideal...

He swore to secrecy of all that had happened - the oath was personally given by the President of India... He was thrilled by his secret meeting with the President - the chief of that secret cell then handed over few papers to him... "Son - we have torn off the papers from your diary for those days - we have carefully - attached new sheets for those days, to keep the secrecy - you are free to leave the security and go back home after you write down those as per these papers..."

Chaits looked at the bunch of sheets which were handed over to him, "Sir - a few moments ago, I took a solemn oath in front of the President to secrecy - and I will abide by my oath..."

"We know you will..."

"But the pages you tore off my diary are my fond memories and I don't want to lose them..."

"I understand - and it's my promise - I will keep them in safe custody and return these pages to you - maybe - after 10 years - once the dust settles down and these pages are no longer relevant. The importance of these papers is high and so will the memory card remain with us - if anyone asks you for details of those days - you have the answers... this is for your own safety..." he pointed at the sheets.

It took Chaits about a week to write those papers handed by the army in his diary and to memorize the chain of events as written in them - to tell the world about them. The truth was deep down his heart and he knew he had to hide it there... He was given a new mobile with new SIM card with the same old number - his mobile was to remain in army's custody for at least 10 years...

He no longer wished to fly - so he was booked in a special coupe of Rajdhani express leaving for Mumbai... A normal taxi covered by some secret agents drove him to the railway station and watched him board the train. Unknown to him there were some secret agents booked in that bogie as passengers and staff guarding him... he looked out as the train rumbled out of the station - back to Mumbai - his hometown... there was no trouble... he seemed to have left the trouble, back in Malaysia.

He soon joined his organization back and the daily activities took the control over. Everything was normal... seems he had moved on...

## CHAPTER THREE

One year later, he was travelling to New Delhi on Rajdhani express for a new project... It was an overnight train journey and looking out of window made no sense as it was dark - with nothing else to do, he double checked his purse for its contents and saw an old memory card he had forgotten about... He changed the memory cards to look at the content it stored... lo! It contained some of his favourite music tracks he had forgotten about... He opened the picture gallery and started scanning the gallery - it contained many old photos - this memory card was about a year old....

He started scrolling through them when one held his attention - Shongita - he had met her at Rajesh's engagement bash. She had been eyeing him right from the moment he had entered and was impressed by his popularity in the team. He had finally won her heart when he had sung few songs in his silky voice... She had unabashedly approached him, introduced herself and complimented him - then onward, it had been a breath taking love affair between them which was cut short when her family had moved to New Zealand...

He wiped off the sweat on his forehead in her fond memory - he started scrolling through the photos again and each photo pushed him to a memory lane and brought a smile on his face - he kept on smiling and scrolling - till he scrolled to a photo - his mind refusing to budge - his eyes, filled with tears... 'LISHA PIEN'...

His memory transported him to events - *One Year ago...*

"Congratulations!!" Christy had shouted across the office as he walked out of his cabin, "Chaits! You made it - Guys - meet the number one sales person of the year..." and he gladly pointed out Chaits... The incentive was mind boggling - an incentive trip to Malaysia and 2000 USD in cash on the touch down... plus he could take along a girlfriend/wife for free...

"Wow! Thanks Boss! and the whole team..." and from that day he was in multiple minds - he could take a girlfriend along with him - which one?

After a lot of thinking - he decided that he won't ask any of his girlfriends - lest - he'd lose others for favouring someone. He wanted to enjoy being the most wanted bachelor boy... everyone advised him to go there and find the best of items before deciding what to buy. The itinerary was sent out and their passports called in for VISA application. All those who had qualified for the trip had nothing else to discuss but the forthcoming trip... when the time was due they packed their bags and reached Mumbai Central station for their Rajdhani express ride - they were about 15 of them from the Mumbai branch...

They all waited patiently for the train to arrive - it was delayed by about 5 hours the railway officials had not given any reason for the delay. About 3 hours later, they saw a buzz and everyone was being escorted out of the platforms. The security personnel started rushing in... They looked at the train arrive on the platform but were bundled out... suddenly everyone's mobiles stared to buzz...

There had been about 5 bomb blasts that had occurred in the city on the local trains and buses - a bomb was supposed to have been planted on one of the platforms... 'Damn the terrorists' they casually cursed... these occurrences were normal to Mumbai...

As the news of more specific locations started to trickle in, their concern for their family and friends who used to frequent those routes grew and each one started to call, to ensure that their near and dear ones were safe and sound...

After scanning all the platforms it was decided that the news of a bomb on the platform was hoax and they were allowed to board the train... Even as the train rumbled out of the station, they were still on calls with their family and friends. Once the train rolled out of Mumbai suburbs, it gained fearsome speed - this was a priority train and the track had been kept free for it to cover the delay... they settled down and had their meals served complimentary on the train after which they could discuss only the terror and the terrorists - *is there no solution to this gangrene of the society*?

They were greeted by a placard outside New Delhi railway station and then led to a bus and bundled into a hotel. They lazed around and greeted their colleagues from different parts of the country, as and when they arrived... as the evening approached, Chaits was in no mood to laze around like others he decided to go out for a stroll - he asked the counter for the directions to the nearest popular market...

"Chaits!" a familiar excited voice called out his name and he turned around... It was Kamal Kaur, his colleague from Chandigarh...

"Hey! Kamal... when did you arrive from Chandigarh?"
"Where are you going?"
"I was getting bored so I decided to go to a popular market nearby - the girl here recommended Karol Baag..."

"Karol Baag? It's a good shopping option - I will join you - I know Delhi pretty well and guide you to shops for what you want to buy... I have my car at your disposal..."

They enjoyed their stroll in the market looking at various goods on display for sale. More than the goods, it was the sense of togetherness as they held hands tenderly - she was glad for Chaits and told him that she had not qualified for the trip - he could have suggested her name as girlfriend and she would have been glad to accompany him as his girlfriend to Malaysia...

"Oh! Sorry - didn't click me - this is what happens when you don't keep in touch regularly - I'd have been glad to take you along as my girlfriend - but, it's too late now - VISA formalities have already been completed..."

"I know - but how could I have suggested you this? Would have looked cheap on my part..."

"There's nothing cheap about it," he put an arm around her shoulder, "aren't you my girlfriend?"

They were driving back to hotel when she suddenly veered off to a side - she could no longer control herself... she leaned over and kissed him sweet, "Go on - enjoy yourself and enjoy on my behalf too..."

She dropped him outside the hotel and drove off - her heartbeats accelerating the speed of her car...

Next day saw them completing all the formalities - travel certificates, cash exchange for USD and were bundled out to the airport after dinner, boarding their flight to Kuala Lumpur...

## CHAPTER FOUR

Chaits looked in wonder at the magnanimous Subang International Airport - they had to wait till immigration formalities were complete - Walking on the conveyor belts they reached the check-in counter for their next flight to Penang...

*Little did Chaits know what this trip had in store for him...*

They were checking their bags in for the flight when Chaits realized that he had a pouch with him that didn't belong to him - he attached the pouch to his waist and asked the tour operator, "How much time do we have to board the next flight?"

"Why?" asked Sudhir their tour operator and guide.

"I need to pee."

"We have 45 minutes to gather here. Those of you who want to pee - the toilets are there - noted as TANDAS - rest you stay here..." he pointed over to the place.

Chaits hurried toward the place thinking hard as to how he had an extra pouch... he remembered, when he was waiting to pick up his bags from the baggage area there was this Pakistani who had travelled in the same plane. He was struggling with number of baggage items and he had looked at Chaits desperately, had requested Chaits to help him... He had handed over the pouch to him when he picked up 2 more bags. Chaits had seen his own bag arrive and had rushed to pick it up and forgotten about the pouch. It had been almost an hour now and Chaits was sure he couldn't search for the person at this massive airport. He decided to carry the pouch along and see what could be done once he settled down at his destination...

They boarded the flight to Penang and were hoarded off to a waiting bus. On the way to their hotel, they passed the magnanimous bridge of Penang over the sea and everyone was awed at the sight. They checked into the Ferrenghi Beach Hotel after thankfully accepting the welcome drink. They all were paired up with a partner except Chaits...

"We expected you to get your girlfriend along - so now you have a room, all to yourself..." Bajpai explained.

"Unless..." chipped in Christy, "you find a local girlfriend to keep you company...

"Well - that's next to impossible..."

"Not really if you know him..." Christy said nudging Chaits who went red in face...

"Aw! Christy - don't damage my good image..."

"I'm not damaging your good image - just suggesting you what you could do..." they all laughed and jested at Chaits' discomfiture... once in the room he looked at the suite and felt that he should have got one of his girlfriends along. He found the bathroom and freshened up to join the others at the dining area...

"Ladies & Gentlemen - we relax today" Sudhir was addressing their group, "Evening - we go to a major seafood attraction here - It's about 12.30PM, after lunch - you can rest or play yourself off at the swimming pool", he said pointing to the direction of the swimming pool inside the hotel premise, "At 7PM - we assemble at the lobby & by 7.30PM, we move - you'll have to arrange for your own transportation - a cab ride will cost you approximately 4 MYR (Malaysian Ringgits) & can ride up to 4 passengers so that may cost you about 1 MYR each..." Everyone started calculating mentally trying to convert Indian Rupee to Malaysian Ringgit... "Further the food & drinks are at your expense..."

Everyone looked at him in wonder. "Ok, don't look at me like this... look at the Itinerary that was sent to you over a month ago...." They looked at each other wondering if they had bothered to go through it....

"Alright - Let me explain - breakfast & one meal included with the stay & city tours along with flights & flight transfers - anything apart from this - you pay extra..."

People calculated of what & how they'd spend. 'Will the money they carried be enough?' That was the question everybody had in their mind... "And yes - I'm extremely sorry - I should have informed this before..." they all looked at Sudhir... "If during travel, someone asks you to help him or her with their baggage - SAY NO - you never know what it contains... There have been instances where people like you tried to help & later got arrested because the bag they carried with them to help the co-passenger contained drugs or weapons. If that happens - it's out of my scope to help you. I hope none of you have helped someone on our way here..."

Cold sweat broke on Chaits. He was aware of strict laws in the Eastern countries... After a tense meal, he rushed to his room & opened the pouch that he'd carried all along from Subang International Airport. He quickly ransacked the pouch for its content. It contained few toiletries a tooth brush, paste, etc. Chaits heaved a sigh of relief. He put them back & decided to dispense off the pouch when his hand touched a squarish soft bulge. He re-emptied the contents & looked around to find a hidden compartment. It contained a paper pouch... His heart beat fast - he hoped that it contained few tissue papers - slowly he opened it - he couldn't believe what he saw. It was a thick wad of local currency he counted it to be 50K MYR & that was huge... he re-bundled the cash & tried re-inserting it in compartment of the pouch but something else was obstructing... he looked inside & found a small paper package - he carefully opened it - it contained a USB & the paper that wrapped had an address in Kuala Lumpur with a telephone number. Chaits was too honest, someone else, would have been greedy, kept the money & forgotten about the pouch... Chaits looked at his itinerary - he had 2 nights stay in Penang after which they move to Kuala Lumpur... keep their extra baggage at Holiday Inn & proceed for a night's stay at Genting Highlands & return to Kuala Lumpur for another 3 nights stay...

'Hmm - I can meet the person when I'm at Kuala Lumpur & return his pouch to him... the poor chap must be going crazy & cursing me or his luck for losing all this money' Chaits thought... He actually wanted to catch up on sleep but was not able to sleep so he put on the TV and started surfing channels he was amazed to find a Hindi movie being telecast on the national network. He was ready with the best of his white shirts that he normally wore on a bottle green trouser. He had his latest pair of comfortable black sports shoes that he'd purchased for this trip - they had a wonderful grip... Seeing nobody in the lobby he looked around and found a sweet girl at the reception - he turned on his charm & approached her...

"Hi!"

"How may I help you, Sir?" she gave a professional smile at him - but her eyes showed, like most of the secretaries in Mumbai - 'She was Impressed'... The secretaries in Mumbai not only were 'Impressed by him' - but they ended up saying 'I'm Pressed by him' after a fantastic date...

"I'm your guest put up in room 507 and I was amazed to watch a Hindi movie this noon."

"Oh! They show them every day. We have lots of people with Indian origin in this country."

"Hmm - that explains it - hey! We're supposed to go to popular seafood place around... would you know where that'd be?"

"Umm - that should be the Eden Seafood Village. It's hardly about 3 miles from here... you go out of this hotel & take a left on the main road & follow the road till you reach the place - no turns..."

"Wow! That's nearby..."

"Ya and try those spicy dishes cooked with special Malaysian fervour - I'm sure - you'd love them..."

Chaits could almost see her mouth, watering at the thought - he smiled at her "Well, do you like the food there?"

"Oh! Ya!" was her instant reply.

"Maybe we could go there & I can treat you to your favourite dish..."

Her tiny eyes widened "Are you asking me out on a date?"

She had a local oriental accent & it was difficult for Chaits to understand whether she was excited or angry at his proposal...

"Oh! I was just asking you to give me company. I'm new around here & don't know the roads. I thought I could treat you for showing me the place around..."

"I wish, I could but I've the evening shift & I'm stuck here till 2 AM..."

"Aw that's not fair. A lovely lady like you should be home by 10 PM latest..."

• 15 •

"I know but my colleague who does this evening shift has asked me for a favour. His daughter is sick & he needs to be by her side..."

"Oh! I'm sorry to hear that..."

Her face brightened, "Perhaps, you can treat me on Sunday - it's my day off."

"I wish I could but, we all would be at Kuala Lumpur on Sunday - maybe next time when I revisit... here's my visiting card, meanwhile, we can keep in touch on the social media sites. By the way I'm Chaits..."

"Hi... I'm Lin" she took his card & put it in her purse, "You can meet Kaz Chan there & tell him that I referred..."

"Katzchan?"

"No - Kaz Chan. He's my brother-in-law & the Event Manager there - he'll offer you the best of services at a discount..."

"Wow - thanks - Lin, are there any rules preventing people skating on the roads here?

"No... Why?"

"I love skating & I got my roller skates with me. That'd also save me some money..."

"Sir, I think your group's gathering there..." Chaits looked at his group arriving...

"Thanks" and he joined his group...

## CHAPTER FIVE

Chaits found his heart beating fast - his charm worked, even in Malaysia....

"What's the name of place we're going?" he asked Sudhir
"Eden Seafood Village"

Chaits suddenly had adventurous spirit rising in him "Gimme a minute" & he rushed back to his room - picked up a small sack that contained his roller skates, hung it over his back & re-joined others...

They were on their way out when Lin called, 'Sir!'

They looked in wonder as Chaits went across to her counter. She smiled & pulled out a lovely rose from the vase next to her & pushed it in Chaits' hand & smiled, "Enjoy your time..."

"Thanks" said Chaits not wanting to meet eyes with Christy or Rajesh...

"You started - eh?" Christy asked putting a hand on his shoulder & then looked at Bajpai "Didn't I hint when we arrived - he can charm any lady - 9 months to 90 years..."

They reached the main road laughing... here again they were odd numbered - one of them had to ride a taxi alone ... Chaits smiled at them, "Lemme take your worries off - I'm carrying my roller skates - from what I understand the place is about 2/3 miles from here & that's nothing, I can skate it out..."

He quickly put on his roller skates & rolled off towards the place. It didn't take much time for him to reach the place while the others were still trying to hire a cab from the hotel...

He waited outside for others to arrive & then decided to look for a convenient place to sit inside the restaurant - he put his roller skates in the sack & hung it over his back - he was amazed to see a long aquarium on both sides as he walked in - a person was escorting him showing various fishes but he was unable to understand what the person was saying...

"Kaz Chan?" he finally asked the escort who looked at Chaits in wonder for a moment & bowed. He pointed a corner to Chaits signalling him to wait & disappeared. He came back with a short hefty guy.

"I'm Kaz Chan - have we met before?"

"Oh! No - in fact your name was referred by Ms Lin & she asked me to meet you when I visit this place..."

"Ms Lin?" he looked at Chaits.

"Oh! She works at the Ferrenghi Beach Hotel & I'm a guest there."

"Oh! Ha-ha-ha - then you are my guest too." he said shaking Chaits' hand profusely in a gesture of warm welcome.

"What was this person showing me in the aquarium?"

"He was asking you to select a fish that you wanted to eat."

"You mean the type of fish I want to eat"

"No-no... You select the fish you want to eat by pointing it - he catches the fish in his net - tells you the cost. If you agree - he takes it to the kitchen to cook for you - if you don't agree - he puts it back & asks you to select another."

"Wow! That's wonderful - but I don't want to eat fish tonight - I can try something else..."

"Ok, no problem - come with me - I'll give you a special seat."

Chaits followed him into the dining area. He looked in wonder - it was huge - Chaits put a figure of about 500 diners at a time & found that his estimate was wrong - the hall seated 1000 diners at a time - Kaz Chan was proudly informing him about the entire setup...

He took him around & gave him a seat next to the stage... "We have a folk show which starts in a short time. Sit here & you'll be able to enjoy the show without disturbance" he waived to a waiter & spoke to him in a language that Chaits didn't understand, anyways - Chaits didn't understand the local language either. The waiter smiled widely showing the entire array of his teeth...

Chaits realized that he'd been given a place on a reserved table. There was one more reserved table next to where he sat - he looked at the entrance to check if his group had arrived... His attention drew toward a small group that entered. It looked as if they wore some sort of uniform - everyone was dressed in shimmering red on the top of black skirts/trousers with a white waist belt... As the group neared - he saw an absolutely beautiful girl walking in the centre of the group, she was not wearing the uniform - Chaits couldn't take his eyes off her...

She was very attractive... that was the first impression of Chaits as the group neared. They went around the stage & sat on the reserved table next to where Chaits sat ... The group relaxed chatting with each other. She was sitting with her back to the stage - almost facing Chaits...

She was close to Chaits for him to observe her - she had an attractive & a beautiful face. She owned natural, lovely-long-shiny-straight hair - they fell gracefully over her queenly shoulders - she wore sparkling earrings that gleamed in the light with every nod of head - her eyes, though small like most of oriental females, were full of life & expressive - she had a hypnotic smile - her skin was supple & smooth - right up to her finger tips & the natural gloss of her skin revelled in the bright lights - her laughter was charismatic & tinkled thousands of romantic bells of any beating heart around...

She was a magnificent dream for any man who saw her - she was dressed in a thin laced prom dress that fit her exclusively, enough to show her curves to an advantage, over which she tied a white belt giving her curves more grace. On the lower half, something that looked like a knee deep swishing skirt worn over a swishing long gown that covered her legs up to her toe...

Chaits looked at her - his mouth wide open - unashamed & unblinking looks - trying to judge - what in her was more attractive & finally decided - she was dramatically beautiful - top to toe... His trance was broken as few people walked on the stage - setting up instruments & chairs...

He saw Kaz Chan walk on the stage & announce the evening programme - Chaits looked at his watch it was about 7PM. They would be playing English band before the main show of local folk music & dance which was to start at 8PM...

His eyes caught up with the waiter & he signalled another mug of beer - he looked back at the attractive table & with beating heart & watched them get up & vanish - but was happy at heart - the beautiful girl he had been admiring had managed to glance back at him - meet his eyes for a quick moment before vanishing - this clearly meant *She Had Noticed Him*...

With nothing else to do - he picked up the menu card & started going through the content - the place was expensive - each mug of beer cost him 9 MYR, add another for a tip meaning 10MYR... His mind suddenly remembered the pouch that he'd accidently carried along with him & felt sad - 'Poor Guy! I hope he has enough money on him for a couple of more days - when I reach Kuala Lumpur - the first thing I want to do is - call that guy & hand him his pouch with all the money.' He was thus brooding over the happening... He didn't even notice the performers walk onto the stage - a sweet voice boomed over & broke the train of his thoughts...

"I'd like to start the evening with this song of ABBA - dedicated to this gentleman who's sitting by the stage & brooding over something..."

Chaits looked at the stage - he forgot everything else... The voice belonged to that beautiful damsel - he'd been admiring not few minutes back - he realized that she was referring to him as she spoke & waived around to the claps that sounded & echoed. She directly looked at Chaits as she started singing 'Chiquitita' from ABBA's album - her sweet voice tinkled every romantic string in Chaits' heart - his sight was completely arrested by her beauty & she held Chaits' attention by raising her eyebrows periodically to completely finish him off with her hypnotic smiles. Chaits imagined his heart develop wings & fly off to that beauty... she was singing this song & had dedicated the same to him...

She continued singing one song after another - most of them were from ABBA or Boney M albums & few of others - Chaits found it rather strange as these were old numbers & none seemed to be from latest...

Then Kaz Chan walked onto the stage & announced that they'd shortly begin with the folk music & dance - once again the troupe vanished.

Chaits had completely forgotten about his group & looked around... Finally, he managed to locate Christy & waived to him - Christy waived back signalling him to sit where he was...

The folk show started - it was an interesting show that revealed rich tradition of the country. He was about to order for his dishes when the smiling waiter got two glasses of wine - Chaits looked at him in surprise as he pulled a chair in respect to a lady who smiled at him & occupied that chair - she then looked at Chaits & smiled sweetly, "I hope you don't mind..."

Chaits looked at her with rising heartbeats - she was the same damsel - she looked fabulous. All the songs she had sung had made her thirsty but she didn't seem tired...

Chaits gave a wide smile "Of course, not" he said, his voice was automatically soft & had the special tone that he always had used to win over those secretaries. "I must say - that you have a heavenly voice & you sing wonderfully well."

"Oh! Thank you." she said blushing at his compliment...

"Hi, I'm Chaits - I mean Chaitanya..." he said introducing in his natural style.

"Hi - I'm Pien" Chaits noted her name mentally & was unsure whether that was her first or last name.

"How long have you been singing like this - I mean here at Eden Seafood Village?" Chaits asked wanting to strike a conversation.

"It's just been 2 days."

"2 days?"

"Yes - Kaz Chan is my brother-in-law & runs the show here - his main singer has on leave - gone to Kal..."

"Kal?"

"Oh! That's short for Kuala Lumpur."

"Oh!" he prodded her to continue - his ears all wanting to hear that sweet voice over and over again…

"I was here at Penang & he knew I can sing - so he offered me a temporary job."

'How many beautiful sisters-in-law did Kaz Chan deal with?' that was a huge question in Chaits' mind, "So - you're not from Penang?"

"Oh! No - dayuhan - I'm sorry - from outside - Philippines - we shifted to Malaysia about a year back when my father got a job with the Government…"

Chaits was looking at her intently - trying to capture her looks, her style & her presence - that was being etched on his heart.

"Where are you from?"

"I'm from Mumbai, India - I'm here on a holiday that I earned" he was proud of his achievement & did not want to hide it…

"Oh! Nice to know that… So are you here, alone?"

"No - I'm with a group of about 35 colleagues - they're sitting around somewhere. So what do you do - I mean apart from singing?"

"I am actually a tour guide & I take tourists to different places in Malaysia - mostly those are families who come here on a holiday - they hire car & my services for sightseeing"

"Do you drive?"

"Yes! - I do - why?"

"Well - you look too young to possess a driving licence."

"I'm 21 years old" she said proudly

"You look only 16."

She was obviously pleased with his remarks & her eyes sparkled as she smiled sweetly at him… They ordered for their food & spoke over the dinner... 'Oh! How I wish, you were our tour guide.' Chaits couldn't help wishing thus...

"No - problem - you can contact me if you come back here - I charge 100 MYR/day of touring. For you - I'll give you a 25% discount."

"Oh! That's so nice of you."

"So - what're your tour plans?"

"I don't remember correctly - but we're here for couple of days more & then we move to Kal visit places around" he explained "then on Sunday evening - the group returns to India"

"Oh! I wish I can meet you before you leave."

"I will call you before I leave."

"Here" she said handing a visiting card to him & he responded by exchanging it with his card - she took the card & put it in a hidden pocket of her waist belt.

Chaits looked around & saw Christy waiving to him to meet the group outside "I gotta go - my group's leaving - if possible - I'll drop in tomorrow again" he said signalling for the cheque to the waiter...

"Oh! No - you don't pay - you're our guest." Chaits looked at her in surprise. "This is the first time you've visited & it's our honour to have a guest like you - the bill is on us." Chaits graciously accepted that "By the way if you're dropping in again tomorrow, please come in around 8PM - I'll be free to chat with you again" she smiled sweetly at him.

He left the place - his heart pounding - the group was outside & Sudhir had invited them to a discotheque 'ON THE HOUSE.' They left for the discotheque - the only thing Chaits found interesting in the discotheque was the toilet - it had animal faces with mouths opened wide - ready to drink whatever was peed into them...

After that - they returned to the hotel & slept - Chaits slept dreaming about his new find - Pien... Tomorrow - they go for a city ride... and Chaits hoped to get the glimpse of Penang Bridge...

# CHAPTER SIX

It was a hectic day to start with. The group was ready at 8AM for the city tour of Penang. It was a normal city tour that showed various places in Penang including the Kashmir corner... They had a good look at the famous Penang Bridge & everyone was clicking happily, capturing the memories of their visit to this country...

As usual, Chaits was busy using his phone camera to capture these images... after which they passed their hotel again & the Eden Seafood village to reach the famous butterfly farm - the place was beautiful & covered with nets. Chaits watched lots of butterfly species even as they flew around - he tried capturing those in his mobile phone camera - but the delay time of the shutter click was too long & he finally gave up the & just watched them...

On their way out everyone was collecting mementos - most of his group settled on purchase of butterfly farm T-shirts - Chaits looked around glum - he had forgotten to change his USD to the local currency...

The tour was short & they returned by noon - having nothing much to do, Chaits decided to explore surroundings...

"What's the plan for the evening?" he asked Sudhir - his heart wanting to go back to Eden Seafood Village & meet Pien again...

"Well, nothing much - actually the visit to Eden Seafood Village was scheduled for today evening - since we had time & its nearby we visited there yesterday - we have tables booked for us at 7.30 PM & the meal is included - any drinks - extra. Chaits' joy knew no bounds - he was going to meet Pien today as well...

"Well, I'll go out then & met you all there. I know the way & I heard that the beach around is beautiful & I like beaches - so I'll go ahead."

"Ok - see ya then at 7:30"

Chaits came back to his room & freshened up - put on his best perfume - Pien- he couldn't shake her off his mind... He was about to leave when he stopped, 'Oh! Let me carry the paper on which the guy's phone number is written along with the address in Kal - poor guy, at least, his mind will be at rest when he hears from me & knows that I'm returning his pouch' he thus thought... He picked up the paper & kept the pouch back in his bag - locked the room & left...

"Hi - Lin!" he greeted her as he approached the reception.

"Oh! Hi... Mister Chaits!"

"Only Chaits"

"Ok - how was your day so far?"

"Well - pretty good - had been for city tour of Penang - I must say that the bridge & the butterfly farm are impressive."

"Ya - they are..." she said proudly - it seemed that everyone in Penang were proud about showing off these two places.

"You know - Lin - I wanted to make a phone call - most probably the number is from Kal - how can I make the call?"

"Oh! You simply dial #9 from your room telephone & then dial the number - but it'll be expensive to use that..."

"Any other way?"

"Yes. When you go out & turn towards left - there're lots of phone shops - you can buy a calling card for 10, 20 or 50 MYR - you'll get a telephone booth near Eden Seafood village - simply insert it - wait 10 seconds & dial the number - it'll keep cutting money till you finish all the money in there - then you buy a new card."

"Oh! You're so sweet & helpful, Lin..." she beamed happily at his compliment even as Chaits moved to the currency exchange counter - the mention of buying a calling card made him remember how he couldn't purchase a memento at the butterfly farm... He put on his roller skates - he stopped at every shop inquiring about the calling card - finally he found a shop & got himself 2 cards worth 10 MYR each - one for contacting the poor guy & the other to call back home in Mumbai - he realised how much he missed his family and his heart saddened when he realised that his group goes back on Sunday while he would have to wait for another week to return... all alone...

He looked around for a telephone booth to make a call - but couldn't find one - what he saw was a group of people far off & then saw one of them enjoy parasailing - 'Oh! Water sports - I wonder what it would cost' - He briskly walked toward them - he saw more people gathering to enjoy water sports & the sea...

Soon, he reached the spot & watched they had 3 different rides - parasailing, water scooter & banana ride... He approached one of the guys & asked for the rates...

"40 MYR - each ride" he replied.

"That's too much - in Goa - I'll get all these rides in 40 MYR."

He pointed to another guy "Mostafa" he called & waived Chaits to negotiate with him... Mostafa gave him a wide smile & shook hands. A similar conversation followed - Chaits wanted to enjoy those rides but Mostafa wouldn't budge with the rates - then Chaits played the card of a group deal & Mostafa yielded "40 MYR - all rides - 15 people..." he agreed in broken English.

"Ok - wait - I'll get the others" & he turned back - came onto the main road - memorised the sign, put his roller skates on & quickly made his way back to the hotel - it was just about 3PM. He called everyone from his Mumbai Team & explained them the deal - everyone was excited - as a courtesy, they informed others & finally it was a group of 30 people who landed on the beach - Mostafa looked at the group & then at Chaits with some amazement "Good Friend" he said, "I keep my promise"

Chaits waited for his turn - after all - he played host - this was his deal...

When it came to his turn, Chaits realized that Mostafa favoured him with lengthier rides & at the end refused money from him, "Good friend, you give me good business - I take no money from you" he said in his broken English, profusely shook his hand & hugged him in joy "You - always welcome - you - friend of Mostafa..."

Chaits returned with everyone to the hotel - he was wet & smelt sea water - freshened up again & rolled off toward Eden seafood village. He was taking off his roller skates when he realised that he'd to call the poor guy whose pouch was with him - he looked around & saw the phone booth - he inserted the card & dialled....

"Hello!" a voice answered the call.

"Hi - can I speak to the gentleman who flew on Saturday night from Karachi to Kuala Lumpur?"

"Sure - what's this about?"

"Well – er - I helped him pick up his bags at the airport. He left a pouch with me in the process."

"Oh! Thank you for calling me - do you still have it?"

"Yes - how can I return it to you?"

"Where are you?"

"I'm at Eden seafood village, Penang"

"Oh! That's alright - I'll arrange to pick that up - how'd I recognise you?"

This seemed pretty easy - he was in Penang as well & will collect it from where Chaits was... "I'm wearing a blue T-shirt on white trousers & Rebok is printed in bold on my T-shirt - I thought you were at Kuala Lumpur & I'm supposed to move there tomorrow - so I called you."

"That's very nice of you - I'll ask someone to meet you there - I'm still at Kal."

"I'm sorry - but I'd like to hand the pouch to you personally - you know how much money is in there..."

"OK - call me when you visit Kal" and he hung up. Chaits was happy - his burden & on his conscience had eased off now his heart was 100% looking forward to meet - Ms Pien... Again - it was around 7PM & Kaz Chan greeted him as he entered the main hall - he was once again, offered the same seat & the whole scene repeated - the only difference - Ms Pien now sat on the same table away from her performing troupe. His heart had more butterflies than those at the butterfly farm counted together as she smiled sweetly at him...

"Hi - Chaits, right?"

"Absolutely - Ms Pien" Chaits joy knew no bounds – 'She remembered him by his name', "I think, I'll have the pleasure to hear you sing tonight - as well..."

"Yes - so it's your last night at Penang - right?"

"Ya - but - maybe - I might return next Monday - er - if you're still here."

She frowned not understanding his plans. "But you said your group is returning to India on Sunday?"

"Hmm - I'm sorry - I forgot to tell you because I was thinking something else - my group is returning - not me - I'll be in this country for another week & no tour plans binding me..." her face brightened, "Maybe, you can be my tour guide for those days..."

"Why not?" she said blushing & excited, "you tell me what you'd like to see around and I'll suggest you some more places."

'I just want to see you & be around with you' Chaits said this in his mind. "Oh! That's wonderful - then - it's decided - for next week you'll be my tour guide - from what I understand, I should be visiting Kal & Genting Highlands - with my group - so you can make a plan & let me know how much will the entire week cost - including our travel, food & your fees..."

She thought for few minutes. "If we rent a car all around that may be costly - how comfortable are you - if you've to take bus or train?"

"Oh! No problems at all - whatever you say..."

"So if we combine car rental & other travel by bus or trains - I'll put that to maximum of about 2000 MYR - including my fees..."

Chaits quickly calculated the money he was carrying - he had about 2500 MYR left - then his face brightened - he was yet to get promised 2000 USD - that clearly gave him another 3000 MYR - this means - he could cover any additional expenses - now he had a wide smile "It's a deal..."

"Excuse me I've to go, the programme starts in few minutes... " she got up & vanished toward the kitchen -

maybe that was the rest room for the performers - the Troupe started off on their music tracks & Chaits got lost - looking at beautiful Ms Pien - after their performance - they ate their dinner together - but this time Chaits insisted on paying the bill & paid a whopping amount of 150 MYR.

"Well, I'll have to go back to singing again" she said smiling sweetly, "We sing after the folk show as well - till 10 - I'll wait for your call & keep the tour plan ready" and she moved on to the stage.

At about 9.30PM - his group had finished their dinner & he joined them outside the place - they had long discussion for what could be the next plan - some of them wanted to revisit the discotheque, some wanted to go back & sleep, while most of them had other plans - they discussed for about 30 odd minutes & separated - the group dispersed according to their plans - Chaits wasn't sleepy - nor was he interested in the plans discussed by the group - he looked up & saw the moon shining brightly. Then he looked at the sea shimmering under the bright moonlight - he loved nature - so he decided to walk back along the beach - he would have to walk just about more than 100 meters before he could hit the beach... "Enjoy yourselves" he said waiving to his group who left & looked at the balance who were inquiring with the waiter near the welcome desk - soon their discussion was over, the waiter hailed cabs for them & they whizzed off... Chaits looked at a rather desolate road ahead then once again at the main entrance of Eden seafood village - took a deep breath - and started walking back to the beach 'See you - Pien - in few more days...'

## CHAPTER SEVEN

Soon he started enjoying his solitude on the desolate road 'This is peace' he thought as he walked inhaling the fresh sea breeze. He reached the point where the beach began & was about to turn left to enter the beach for the walk on the sand when he stopped, "Hey! Chaits!" a female called him. He looked around & saw someone riding a bicycle from behind - he was wondering who'd know him by his name in Penang & had to wait for the person to reach him...

"Chaits!" the voice called again & he instantly recognised - Pien.

"Hey! What are you doing here?"

"I ride back to the Hotel - my sister works there - I sit & while my time around till she finishes her duty & then the hotel car drops us back to our home."

"And the bicycle?"

"We put it on the top of the car & get it down when we reach."

Chaits was now almost accustomed to the broken English of Pien - even as they spoke a car stopped by - it was her troupe.

"So what are you doing here?"

"Well - I'd nothing much to do - so I decided to walk back to the hotel along the beach - the moon as bright & lovely"

"Which hotel?"

"Ferrenghi Beach Hotel."

"Oh! Then let me walk along with you. That's where my sister works."

"What about the bicycle?"

She turned around and spoke to her troupe in their local language - they put her bicycle on the top of the car, waived bye & drove off...

Chaits looked at her - the moonlight highlighted her beauty - all the more & his heart flip-flopped as she smiled at him - he couldn't resist looking & measuring her up - top to toe - "Ms Pien!!" he exclaimed. "What happened to your dress? - I mean this was a nice gown - did you cut it off?"

She looked amused & burst out laughing "No - it's detachable - I took the lower part off so that I can ride my bicycle..."

"Oh!" Chaits couldn't take his eyes off the shapely legs that shown below the knee long skirt...

"Didn't you go along with your friends?" she asked casually.

"No - I didn't like their plan."

She raised an eyebrow & intently looked at him, "I know they planned to pick up chicks for the night."

Chaits looked at her - embarrassed "I'm sorry - we did come here as a group - but that doesn't mean that I've to do what they do..."

"I'm surprized - I thought you love to be among females - at least you look flirty."

Chaits smiled "Ya - people think I'm flirtatious - but I'm not - I'm just plain - Friendly"

"You're a man - and you'd definitely love to have sex..." now that was a bold & direct statement.

"I'm not sex crazy - sex happens to me by accident - especially when the emotions of my female friends go over board - I hate paying for sex - there's no emotion there - plain exchange of your money for releasing your frustration - I hate that - I like friends around me - real people with real emotions for me..."

"Oh! That's very nice" she smiled broadly at him, "You know, you're different from others - that's why I like you." she extended her hand out to him "Friends?"

He shook her hand, "Friends..." and they started walking on the beach...

"Ms Pien..." Chaits was interrupted

"Lisha - Lisha Pien - that's my name - only friends are allowed to call me - Lisha - you're allowed to call me - Lisha."

"Ok - Lisha..." Chaits smiled, "Lisha - you agreed to be my guide - I'm alone & unmarried & as you said - err - flirty..."

She smiled sweetly, "Yes - you're flirty - but a nice person - and I know you'll not cross you limits."

"How do you know that?"

"Ever heard - a woman's instinct...?" Chaits wondered what she meant... "So - this is the first time I'm going to be a guide to a lone man & not a family, because I trust you & besides, I know, I can take care of myself."

Chaits couldn't make a head or tail of what she spoke. This happened to him every time she spoke a lengthy sentence in her thick oriental accent in broken English - he diverted the topic...

"Tell me what you will show me after I meet you on Monday - by the time I'll know, what I've seen..."

"We will start from Air Itam & see the Kek Lok Si temple at Bukit Bendera" they walked on as she started explaining how she'd start with surrounding places to Penang & go forth from there - Chaits couldn't understand her planning, after all - he was visiting Malaysia for the first time. He was simply engrossed in her sweet voice. They'd have walked for about 15 minutes when they stopped & stood still for few moments looking at the beauty of shimmering sea & feeling the cool sea breeze - Chaits was finding it hard to resist putting an arm around her shoulder - but was in two minds - should he or should he not ... His want got better of him & he was about to put his arm around her when he heard someone speak from behind...

"So you managed to get a girl for the night" the man said in broken English, "We always fight for the honour of local girls here - you managed to take advantage of such a sweet girl..."

"We're friends "Chaits explained, "she was telling me - how beautiful this country is..."

"Then why are you here with her on this lonely beach?"

"I was walking all by myself & she joined me. There's nothing like what you think."

"That's true." Lisha asserted.

"Oh! No no no - we know bastards like you. The only way we can let you go - is - let the girl come along with us and give us everything you carry - and we'll let you go - no harm..."

"We?" Chaits wondered aloud & he saw a group of 5 more join this guy - one of them was huge about 6'5" & broad - the rest were normal height about 5'7" tall but well built - Chaits thought for a moment, 'If these people were really concerned about Lisha, they'd have asked her to come along with them - why the hell were they asking him to hand over his belongings - overall they've not spoken to Lisha at all - they could've easily clarified with her in the local language than threatening him in broken English - these are, but common thugs.' he concluded. He sized them up. He was sure - he'd be able to deal with them but the big one was a doubt - he was concerned about Lisha's safety...

"I'll give you nothing - and the girl - she goes with me..." Chaits said in a firm voice & Lisha looked at him in surprise...

"It's alright Chaits - I'll go with them - they would harm you..." she said.

"We just decided - we're going to be friends - does a friend leave you when you need him the most? - not me..."

Even as they argued, three of them blocked the way behind Chaits - two of them blocked each side - the huge guy stood behind Lisha - preventing any possibility of escape - Chaits carefully studied their formation - his natural instincts of a fighter & the hard training for his boxing during college days suddenly was prominent in his attitude & stance...

"Run - Lisha" he shouted as he turned - hit the first man a solid right hand upper-cut on his jaw which sent him reeling - knocked out. He balanced himself & kicked the other one - hard on his shin - the speed & impact was so much that the guy lost his footing & fell flat - face first... He moved his right hand opposite way & hit the next one on his temples - that was a fearful blow again & that man reeled as well - knocked out.

He ducked clearly avoiding the punches that came his way - instinctively & turned on them, then followed a small melee of hands & feet flying around - soon - the five lay on the beach - either knocked out or dazed by the speed of Chaits' attack - he quickly looked around - to his dismay - Lisha was still standing there - watching him ground his opponents - not realizing that the huge man was behind her, extending his arm to grab her...

"Lisha run..." Chaits shouted - desperately making his way toward the big man. The big man was ready for him - he quickly stepped aside & grabbed Chaits - lifted him by his waist & threw him few feet away - Chaits was mad at the big guy - never had he been thrown around in this fashion during the championship - he got up - brushed the dust off him & walked toward the big man - he knew - the big man was quick & had tremendous strength. They slowly circled - poised - waiting for the other to make the first move. Chaits started dancing back & forth in the famous boxing stance - the big man suddenly lashed a kick at him... Chaits evaded his kick 'To hell with boxing rules' he said to himself & punched the big man's shin - hard... The big man obviously felt the pain of his box as he stumbled trying to regain his balance which brought his face within the punching distance & Chaits took the opportunity & punched away in quick succession at his face & followed with a fierce kick behind his knee buckling him up & then planted a fierce upper-cut on his jaw - the big man reeled & fell on the beach - Chaits was about to deliver another kick in his mid-rib....

"Watch out! Chaits!" Lisha shouted, Chaits turned around & faced the two who had recovered from his initial attack - this time - they were ready - but soon proved hopelessly overpowered by Chaits' strength & speed. They lay at his feet - knocked out...

After all of this - Chaits was a bit tired but had enough strength & energy to carry on - he was not concerned about the five who lay senseless around him - but the big guy was a concern - he'd recovered & too quickly, he was charging at him...

"**Haaa-yiii-yeeahh**"

Chaits stood there - stupefied by the kick that followed the classic martial arts cry... He couldn't believe what happened - his mind lost all its thoughts. His hands & feet refused to move - he just looked on... Lisha had suddenly moved... She was about 2ft high from the ground & performed a classic mid-air split - her leg toward the ground folded as her other leg was straight - 180°- up in the air... she hit the big man straight on his face with a fierce kick & she landed perfect - after a somersault. All this happened in a split second. The big man looked at Chaits for a moment - his eyes froze & he fell backwards - senseless!!

"Wow! Lisha! - that was fantastic!"

She looked at Chaits - content with his amazement "Thanks to my Kung Fu training - I'm a black belt. I have been learning & developing this skill for almost 7 years now" she said proudly - Chaits had not yet got over with the amazement & looked at her in awe...

"Sorry - I didn't help you at first. I was checking your fighting skills & style - I must say you're GOOD - and pretty fast."

"Aw - that's nothing compared to you."

"No - I mean what I said, I could've easily put them down all by myself but I was trying to understand your style - is this some kind of Kung Fu that is practised in India?"

Chaits started laughing "No."

"Why are you laughing?"

"Because - this was not Kung Fu..."

"But - your style was wonderful. What was it?" she still didn't want to let go the topic.

"It was boxing - I've been the Inter-college champion for three successful years and the kicks were Football..."

She started laughing with him & her laughter melted Chaits' heart completely. He could feel it beating fast - to control his emotions he looked away from her toward the road - to his horror he saw a group of another 10 people running toward them - "Shucks" he exclaimed & braced for another brawl...

Lisha looked in the direction & stopped laughing - she held Chaits' hand "Let's run & disappear into the darkness." They started running away from the approaching group - but stopped in their track as they saw another group of about 20 odd people approach from the end - they were running into...

"Shucks!" Chaits exclaimed again "Lisha - I think you better run for it while I engage these guys..."

"Sorry Chaits! Did you leave me alone when they first approached? - now it's my turn..." Chaits looked around desperately - he now knew Lisha's fighting skills & was confident about tackling 15-20 of them along with her - but they seemed to be far outnumbered now... He braced himself ready for action to follow... They faced the first group of about 10-12 men as they poised for the attack 'What are they waiting for? Others to join?' Chaits was in two minds to attack - or wait for attack.

"Hey! What's happening here?" a voice called out from the group of 20 odd people who were approaching from the other side - clearly they didn't belong to these thugs and the voice was familiar. Chaits looked at the group...

"Oh! It's my friend, Chaits!" the voice sounded excited as the man approached - as he neared - moonlight allowed Chaits enough vision to recognise him...

"Mostafa!"

"Yes - Mostafa - what's happening?"

"These people want my money & my friend here - we were just walking on the beach."

"Is that so? Take the girl along with you - we'll deal with them." Chaits looked at him. "Go-on" he prodded & signalled to his men who rushed at the other group even as Mostafa pushed Chaits & Lisha to go away...

Chaits saw this opportunity to take Lisha to the hotel - safely - he grabbed her hand "C'mon - let's go..." and they ran from there - soon they stood - huffing & puffing at the hotel entrance - Lisha bent on him for support & he couldn't stop himself caressing her soft & shiny hair...

"Thank you - Chaits" she smiled at him, "this never happens here - I wonder who they are..."

"Never mind" he said happy that they both were safe & thanked Mostafa for showing up on time - he'd definitely go & meet him, to thank him personally before he left Penang tomorrow afternoon... They entered the hotel lobby where Lisha quickly told her sister 'Lin' of her adventure...

"Oh! Thank you so much - Mr Chaits - that was so kind of you." she said with concern...

Chaits bade them 'Good Night' & left for his room - the first thing he did was to get into a hot water bath to ease off the sore points in his body caused by the brawl...

## CHAPTER EIGHT

The next morning, the first thing Chaits did was to go to the beach, search for Mostafa. He found him & thanked him for his timely help & returned with a feeling of having made a good friend on this foreign land - after lunch, they packed up & left for the airport - Lisha was waiting for him at the airport - they spoke for few minutes before saying 'bye' to each other - on an instinct she hugged Chaits before he vanished to the check-in counter...

He returned to his group - his heart beating fast - he could sense it - this was not a normal friendly hug - it had deeper feelings concealed within... Christy & others enjoyed pulling his leg on this matter, but Chaits was too engrossed in controlling his feelings for her - more than his feelings - he was concerned about her safety - what if those thugs harm her for what wasn't her fault? - but the plane had now taken off & was taking him miles away from her - further, he realised that his visa was only for a specific period... after his visa expires - he'll have to return to India & thereafter he may never be able to meet her again - he hoped that she'll be safe till he returns to Penang - at least, he'd be able to spend a week in her wonderful company.

His plane landed & he walked confidently on somewhat familiar - Subang International Airport - like always, Sudhir helped them clear paper work & formalities & herded them off to a waiting bus. They checked in at Holiday Inn resort on a busy road in the heart of Kuala Lumpur - on arrival everyone was excited & wanted to see around - even if it was growing dark - they ventured out & asked people around - they wanted to check out a local food joint where they could taste the local food - finally they reached some place which seemed similar to the Chowpati in Mumbai - this Chowpati had various dishes at low rates & offered local food cooked in sesame oil - one could smell it from almost a mile... The names to all dishes were unknown - so Chaits settled down for noodles - he watched the procedure in wonder as well at the equipment used to prepare them - Fresh!! Though odd in taste as he wasn't accustomed - he found it - filling...

Sudhir was addressing the group about the plans "I'll request you to split your baggage into 2 parts - we'll be leaving early morning tomorrow - we carry light bags with enough clothes for one night - the main baggage - we deposit here in the hotel lockers - that way your baggage will be safe..."

"Why? And - where are we going?" Sudhir frowned at the interruption to his flow "We leave for Genting Higlands - it's the largest Casino in Asia - it's advisable that you keep your valuables & cash here & carry only the amount you need at Casino or at the bar to buy your drinks. Trust nobody & Do Not Lend your money to anyone you don't know - do not accept drinks offered by any stranger - there've been incidences that the drinks were drugged & people robbed - Gambling addiction is dangerous as you know..."

They all went back to the rooms & followed Sudhir's instructions - Chaits had never been to a casino - gambling is banned in India. Chaits was excited at the thought of visiting a casino. He thought about it & counted & recounted his money - he now had a fair idea about the cost generally associated with beers & other drinks - Finally - he decided to carry about 500 MYR with him & spend only 100 MYR at casino...

When he was thus splitting what he needed, his sight fell on the pouch, 'Oh! My God!' he thought, 'I forgot to call the guy - It's too late now. Let me keep this here in the hotel locker - lest I'm robbed by someone at the casino' - so he put the pouch back - but retained the paper with the address & telephone number scribbled on it...

Next morning, he grabbed a heavy breakfast - he wasn't sure if 500 MYR would suffice - They boarded the tour bus & were soon on their way, Sudhir gave them whatever information he had about the city & places as they passed on "Kuala-means-Kala or Black & Lumpur-means-river, the river that flows through the heart of the city is muddy & blackish in colour - so the name of this city is derived "he kept on feeding the group with tits & bits of information - soon they left the city behind & after sometime they approached mountainous terrain - after climbing a winding road for some time they stopped at the spot - Sudhir beckoned them to alight the bus - everyone gladly alighted stretching their bodies & looked around at the serenity of the nature...

"We've 2 options" Sudhir declared, "1) go by road – 2) Take the ropeway..." Unanimous decision was the ropeway - "the bus will get your bags." he said.

They had to take turns by forming smaller groups & had to wait at least 15 minutes for one group to board - Chaits watched the beauty - he was awestruck... It was a hilly region with forest sprawled around it - the top of the mountain was not visible as clouds shrouded it & the ride on the ropeway was breath-taking. Oh! How he wished to be here with Lisha - this was a perfect setting for romance - he decided that next week when Lisha would be his guide, he'll visit this place again & started daydreaming...

He loved the place & the hotel instantly & his decision was made - he'd definitely come back with Lisha - as they checked in, he carefully studied the rates & found them reasonable, the rates at the restaurant & bars were also reasonable 'Hmm' - he thought, 'nice way to lure suckers to the casino with reasonable rates - they know - people will spend far more, than what they spend on food, bar & the lodging.'

He was a bit unsure about how much would it cost to get Lisha from Penang to Genting & back via Kuala Lumpur - thinking thus - he suddenly got miserly & decided he'd spend only 50 MYR - max at the casino - especially when he saw the photos of the casino outside with slot machines - he'd seen these in the movies...

They had few hours to kill before they met for dinner & then had a go at their luck with gambling in the casino - he loitered around inside the complex - he spoke to the staff trying to know about the place through their broken English. He understood that casino had a dress code for guys - either a blazer or locally manufactured Batik' shirt - he had neither - he was guided to the shopping complex where he found Batik' shirts on sale in abundance - after trying to negotiate a comfortable price - he played the group card again & it worked - he rushed back & informed the group who was angry at Sudhir for not informing them. Every one of them had carried blazers but kept them in the lockers of the hotel back at Kuala Lumpur...

So all of them who wanted to enter the casino entered the shop & purchased the Batik shirts. Chaits always wanted to look different & looked at what others had bought &

selected one that had orange shade - though he hated the colour as a shade of a shirt - but he'd be the only one in the group with this shade - they scrambled back to their respective rooms - donned these ... after that - he didn't want to go up & down the floors & waste precious time of exploration. Chaits wore that Batik shirt to get accustomed to the colour...

He felt bad that he didn't get any of his girlfriends along - he'd been booked - single in every room they stayed & couldn't share his excitement or discuss anything - he didn't have a partner to share his room - having nothing much to do he ventured out again - he carried 200 MYR along with the phone calling cards & the number he needed to dial - he would be returning to Kuala Lumpur - the next day...

He first entered the restaurant & sipped on the English tea! This enabled him to change the big notes into smaller denominations. After which he started loitering again - 'I am sure, I've seen some telephone booths around' - Finally - he located the booths...

"Hello" he same voice answered his call

"Hi - I called you because I wanted to inform you that I'll be in Kuala Lumpur - tomorrow and I want to return that pouch to you."

"Oh! That's so kind of you - by the way where are you?"

"I'm at Genting Highlands"

"Great! I too am visiting the place - my only problem is - I'm very bad at remembering people by faces - what are you wearing?"

"It's a Batik shirt, orange in colour..."

"Good! I hope to reach there by 10PM - which room - I want to thank you..."

Chaits gave him the room number - the guy seemed to be too excited to allow a conversation & kept thanking Chaits profusely - in between Chaits managed to inform that he'd be in the casino & not in his room "Ok-ok! I'll meet you there" and cut the call...

Chaits thought for a moment & put himself into his shoes 'Ya - even I'll be excited if I lost so much money & someone tells me that he's meeting me to return it - don't blame him for that..." He wandered around asking questions to find someone friendly enough to talk to - finally he managed to find an aged waiter who was happy to chat with him...

"Have you ever been into the casino?"

"Yes - I was the bar tender there till a couple of months back. I used to get big tips when people used to win & if they lost - I used to do a good business as a bar tender"

"So - what happened?"

"The management decided to keep girls there now... There are many girls who work in the casino."

"As bar tenders?"

"Yes - the new joiners are bar tenders."

"What about others?"

"The more experienced are promoted as paid companions."

"Paid companions?"

"This is a new concept which gives this setup additional money. Listen you seem to be a good guy so I'll advise don't talk to these girls."

"Why?"

"The setup runs like this - normally, most of the visitors are single males, and they are deep into gambling - most of them lose money here, you may win occasionally here - but you got to be exceptionally lucky to win. If you're a regular visitor you'll know, but the trend is - when you win - they take a deposit of 100 MYR & allow you to play more & offer you free drinks... You're young & you'll know that when you start drinking & win - your logic goes for a toss - and then you play more - till you lose everything..."

"Hmm - nice business idea..."

"And when you lose - you need an emotional support - these ladies then join you, comforting you for a fee of 10 MYR an hour & keep prodding you on to play more, 'Maybe, with me by your side, you may win - I've been a lucky charm for many' - that's the standard line they use... they approach you if they feel you got more money to lose. There's bank inside the casino that allows you to withdraw money or deposit money against your bank account."

"Wow! What a setup - only a win-win situation for the setup. Do you never enter the Casino - now?"

"Not much - but on days where we've a large crowd - I get good overtime money as a bar tender - today is such a day & I'll be bar tending..."

"Oh! Nice to know that - err - what's your name?"

"Abdul."

"Alright - I'd like to make a deal with you."

"What?"

"You're a nice man - yourself - so I've decided that I'll not use any of those paid lucky charms. I want you to be my lucky man Friday - I've decided that I'll play & gamble in the casino for up to 50 MYR from my pocket - I'll increase the amount to 60 MYR - you keep a watch on me... I know - I'm going to lose & I'm prepared to lose 50 MYR for fun of gambling - you help me control the instincts if I start getting carried away - I'll pay you that extra 10 MYR."

"Oh! That's very kind of you!"

"If I win - you never know - I'll pay you all the 60 MYR that I've planned to spend here - they'll all be yours."

His eyes brightened up with the prospect of all that money, "Don't worry, Son - I'll help you & pray for you… what's your name?"

"Chaits."

"At what time will you start bartending inside the casino?"

"My duty here ends at 8.30PM - then I take about 30 minutes to eat my food & change uniform - I should be there about 9.15 PM."

"Great - then see you at the casino bar."

"Bye" he said smiling at Chaits, hoping he'd win - then he'll be able to collect entire night's tips in one go if Chaits keeps his word. Chaits joined others at the dining table & shared the info except his deal with Abdul…

"Oye! Thank you." Bhupi Singh said his eyes wide with lust, "do these girls also give you company in bed?"

"Well - I'm sorry - I didn't ask that - maybe you can ask those girls - yourself." Chaits suggested with a suppressed smile, "but - beware - they might kick your balls off with karate kick - Just like in those Kung Fu movies." the entire group laughed as Bhupi considered Chaits' words & odds…

# CHAPTER NINE

Chaits had entered the casino for the first time & the dazzling lights with the engrossed crowd fascinated him, 'Hmmm - just as they show it in the movies' - he started walking around. First he wanted to grasp the entire view & check out all gambling rigs in there - he loitered around few tables trying to understand the rules of those - he tried but couldn't understand how 'black jack' was played - he wandered off to the next table & felt comfortable they were playing 'bridge' - he knew the game & watched them play - he knew how to play this game, he needed a partner who he could rely on - just picking up someone in the crowd could ruin him - on few questions he understood that these were high stake games & he was content in watching others play - the minimum stake was more than the maximum he wanted to spend.

He strolled on & saw poker being played - now - he knew this game of 5 cards the best - not that he'd gambled before - it was in the digital diary he owned, before he got a mobile phone - it had 'poker' as an entertainment & he used to win - every time… he had not thrown away the digital diary and used to play the game…

Again, the stakes were high, he watched it with interest as he watched the people who played - as more he looked - he found it easier to predict which player would win - he watched about 10 deals & predicted the winner correctly

- his heart desperately wanted to play the game but he resisted it by thinking about his week ahead with Lisha - that was what he wanted the most... With heavy heart he strolled on - he came to a counter & watched housie played with a stake on it. He looked at his watch - 9.30PM.

'Hey! Abdul must be here - bar tending - let me find him' he asked the direction toward the bar & set out to meet Abdul. He looked at lot of girls in a typical uniform - who first looked 'Impressed by him' but later turned their interest to someone else who played & was on winning streak - obviously, the sense of duty & the want of money prevailed over their personal likes & dislikes... He found Abdul at the bar smiling away at every tip he received & generously lending his ear to his customers - he seemed to be excellent at it...

"Welcome, Sir!" he said, "what drink will you prefer?" he smiled as he looked at Chaits.

"I'll like to get a mug of beer." Chaits said smiling back at him.

Chaits was sitting at the end of the bar, Abdul walked over, "It's big business here tonight, sorry, I may be preoccupied - just keep your senses, Son. Normally, we serve strong beer - I got a mug of mild one for you - next time you order - specifically ask for the mild one..." he whispered over to Chaits as he collected cash for the beer - it was cheap- 2 MYR only!! Chaits looked around & found his group already at the slotted machines "Where's the token counter?"

Abdul pointed to his left - good, to reach the counter - he had to pass Abdul's bar - he reached over to the token counter...

"What would you be playing, Sir?"

"I think I'll like to start off with the slot machines."

"That counter, Sir"

Chaits approached the counter - the tokens were 1 MYR each - he pulled out 20 MYR & exchanged them for tokens "If I remain with tokens, what do I do?"

"You can cash your tokens on the other side."

Chaits crossed over to check where... It was a neat setup - as you enter the token counter hall, you bought tokens at counters on your right, and you cash in your tokens on your left - next to cash tokens were bank counters... Chaits got out of the token counter room. He found Abdul glancing at him. He put up 2 fingers in a position that normally looked like 'V' for victory for anyone who saw - Abdul understood - 2 for 20 MYR as he watched Chaits walk toward the slot machines. Chaits was in no hurry to finish his 20 coins, to stop himself from rushing in - he put the snap of Lisha he'd clicked on his mobile when she sang Chiquitita for him - it helped in curbing his desire for gambling - he needed his money to spend a week with her...

He selected a slot machine & waited for the guy to finish his turn - when his turn came - he put his coin in & pulled the lever - after a short time - the flickering lights stopped & he had lost!!

He went from one machine to another that had different games & kept losing his coins - he approached the another machine & put his hand in the pocket - he realized - it was the last coin- in less than an 30 minutes - he'd spent almost 20 MYR - he shook his head & shook the coin as if he was trying to wake up his sleeping fortune - he put the coin in knowing he was going to lose this one as well - he looked at the flickering lights in dismay as they slowed in frequency - of 3, he had 2 highs - it was still searching for third and it passed off even as the search slowed – considerably. Chaits knew, deep down his heart, luck had run out on him even on this machine - he decided to go back & sip a beer. He almost turned around and stopped as the machine suddenly made a sound - he looked at the machine & the sound of it dispensing tokens seemed very sweet - he had hit the Jackpot!!

He watched with beating heart as the machine dispensed 2500 tokens - he pulled out a small sized folding bag - he collected the coins & walked toward the bar, then thought over & entered the cash counter. He cashed 30 tokens - the guy at the counter looked at his balance tokens & said, "You need to deposit 100 more!

Chaits handed him 100 more against which he received a plastic badge, "You can cash this on your way out - it's just a deposit toward any Lucky Charm that you may hire you're now entitled to free drinks here - wear this badge for your free drinks."

Chaits put the badge on his shirt & put the deposit token in his pocket - suddenly all those girls who had taken their interest off him started giving him coy looks - it was his turn to look disinterested...

"Oh! Good! So you won." Abdul said with a smile, "what would you like to drink?"

"Mild Beer"...

Chaits kept his word & handed at tenner to Abdul who smiled in joy "Be careful, son - I would love to have 50 more." Chaits nodded & again moved over to the slot machines - he looked at the 20 MYR note & put it back in his pocket, 'Now - it doesn't matter - whether I win or lose the balance in this bag' he thought, 'I am going to gamble with the money I won at this casino - my hard earned money is safe in my pocket' - he looked at Lisha's photo & kissed it for luck.

He started playing the slot machines again - this time the luck was indeed on his side - the next couple of hours saw him win 5000 MYR apart from the 50 MYR he had promised Abdul. He now wanted to try the higher stake at poker & changed his tokens over to play that game... it was sometime before he saw people lose & get up from the table - the table broke off for 15 minutes to allow players to get fresh tokens & a drink...

When the table re-started, players had declared pack up & Chaits got his turn to play. Initially - he lost about 500 MYR till he managed to read the bluffs & then started playing the bluffs - his way... Everyone was stunned at the way he won - he had 25000 MYR in his kitty now - he felt a need to freshen up.

"I'll be back in 30 minutes" he declared. & cashed 20000 MYR & kept 5000 MYR tokens - he came back to his room & freshened up - opened his bag & prepared a wad of his winnings & pushed that wad - deep inside - neatly hidden by his clothes he made sure that the door to his room was securely locked & returned to the casino with his tokens of 5000 MYR - he was happy - he had additional 20K MYR to spend with Lisha. He had to wait for the poker table to take the break so that he could join if anyone quit... he looked at what players held & knew that it'd take at least 30 more minutes more for the table to break-up...

He returned to the bar where Abdul served another mild beer, "So - you're still winning, eh?"

"Ya - I am safe as far as per profit & loss is concerned."

Abdul laughed & cautioned, "Be careful, son, I think they're now going to send their best girl - Laila, to distract your attention - so that you lose..."

"Thanks for tipping me..." Chaits said handing over another tenner, "how do you know?"

"I can see her approaching - she's alone & on lookout - she's not interested in anybody else - she's almost here..." and he walked away to serve others...

Chaits quietly sipped at his beer, he looked in mirror of the bar display & saw a lady approach - she seemed fabulous & walked in confidence as if she walked on a ramp, swaying her buttocks to lure any man into compromise... "Excuse me" she said in a sweet, sexy, husky tone," is it ok if I sit next to you?"

Chaits turned around feigning surprise, "Oh! Sure - why not?"

"Thank you" she said smiling at him. Chaits couldn't stop himself from looking at her - shamelessly - from her head to toe - measuring her body to a millimetre - she was dressed in the 'Lucky Charm Girl' uniform like other girls in the casino - the diffcrence was in her beauty & attractiveness, in the way her dress which was stitched to show off her curves more exclusively and her soft, sensuous husk tone coupled with an expression of physical want in her eyes - had Abdul not warned, Chaits could've easily fallen to this bait... Chaits mustered up all his will & looked away from her & sipped his beer...

"Oh! Gosh! I'm so tired..." she said in her husky voice - looking at Chaits... she was a bit frustrated as Chaits still ignored her - she kept a soft hand on Chaits' shoulder, "Need a companion?"

"No. I'm alright" he said still concentrating on his beer.

"Excuse me for a quick minute" she said & walked off to her reporting counter - as soon as she left, Abdul approached Chaits with another mug of chilled beer... "Good show, son "he looked pleased, "I swear, I've not seen a single man turn her off - good going - but it stumps me." Chaits looked at his puzzled face, "I heard her control desk people speak - they wanted her to approach some other sucker - maybe- she approached you by mistake - they are pointing out that sucker to her now. It's almost 3AM & I think, It's time for you to call quits - my duty here ends in another 30 minutes - if I stay back, questions will be raised..."

Chaits looked at him "I understand please get me another beer by the time I cash these tokens" Abdul smiled & walked off even as Chaits gulped at his mug & went off to cash his tokens, glad at heart - he'd have about 30K MYR to spend when he'll be with Lisha...

"Wouldn't you be playing more, Sir?" the counter guy asked him anxiously.

"No - I'm sleepy - maybe tomorrow..." the guy gave him 5000 cash along with deposit of 100 MYR.

Chaits came back to Abdul's counter who promptly served him beer & gleefully accepted the gracious tip of 100 MYR that Chaits gave...

A soft hand tapped Chaits on his shoulder, "Hey you're a tough nut to crack".... It was Laila again - this time, her eyes had a twinkle & she didn't seem to fake it - she seemed in genuine want of Chaits' company & her eyes did show that expression of 'Impressed' by him... Chaits had a good look at her & she boldly allowed shameless scanning done by Chaits' eyes of her well-toned body that seemed more voluptuous due to skimpiness of her dress... 'She's no doubt - attractive - nay I'd like to say she's downright - sexy' Chaits thought as he still scanned her shamelessly...

She wore a skimpy golden yellow attire - more than a dress - what she wore looked more like a two-piece designer bikini - her cleavage showed prominently - she had a thick, shiny gloss of medium length hair with a tint of auburn that fell gracefully on her back, over her shoulder and neck & heaving breasts - as if ready to tickle them with a soft touch - a soft transparent golden cloth sprewn with golden stars tried to cover her stomach & abdomen. Similarly her beautiful, shapely legs under were covered, in form of a transparent pajama up to her knee length... she wore golden sandals with a pointed high heels - through her shiny gloss of hair, golden designer ear-rings seemed to peep out and tease any beating heart who watched her - Chaits found his heart beating fast as more he looked at her. Her eyes definitely had an inviting look beneath well carved eyebrows...

"Well", he said slowly, "I'm quits for today - not playing anymore."

"It is ok." she said in her sexy voice, "my duty is over as well." Chaits looked at her - she smiled, "I know - you have a doubt on me - but I can't help it - it's my job to be a 'Lucky Charm Girl - but please understand - I've feelings of my own I even I need to talk to people."

"Don't you charge people for giving them a company?"

"I don't. The management does - we get 10% of that & whatever tips that clients offer - we get a salary for this job."

"Hmmm" Chaits wondered at the setup.

"You're not going to be charged anything for sitting & chatting with me now - I was impressed by your looks & confidence - the moment you entered - but, I had a job at hand..."

Chaits tried & remembered her 'Impressed' looks when he initially stood by the 'Black Jack' table... He looked at her & found the same genuine looks as their eyes met...

"Well, I'm sorry to doubt you to this way - let me make up - let me buy you a drink" her face lit up...

"I'll have whatever is your choice." Abdul had been within hearing distance & had heard every sentence, "Two mild beers, please" Chaits said, Abdul rushed to get the mugs & winked at Chaits...

"By the way, I'm Laila" she introduced extending her hand.

"Hi - I'm Chaits"

"Laila - can you stand over there - I'd like to click a picture of you - for my memories..." she smiled and obliged - she was about 10ft away as Chaits looked at her through the screen of his mobile phone camera.

Taking advantage of this chance Abdul got the mugs. "It's ok - I checked - she's signed off for today" he whispered, "and thanks for your generosity" & he walked off.

"Hey - Laila - come a bit closer - that's it - wait..." he clicked a photo, "thank you, Laila - come - let's enjoy the beer..."

She walked seductively & sat next to him - making sure that her knee gently touched him... he could feel his feelings rise as her knee gently played with his thigh... "Laila - that's an Arabic name - and you don't look Arabic." Chaits wondered.

"Malaysia is a country of diversified cultures that have mixed & mingled with time, people all over Asia settled down here during colonial British regime - so you'll come across lot of names - they could be Arabic like mine, you'll have names from India, China, Singapore, Thai, Filipino, British as well European..."

"For a lucky charm girl - you've good knowledge and can talk smart & interesting" Chaits said with a smile.

"Ya - have to keep up - meet lots of suckers from various backgrounds - sometimes - it's interesting - most of the time it's boring - all they want to do is touch me & want me to go to bed with them."

"Do you go to bed with them?"

"Occasionally - not always - I get a bonus for doing that apart from a hefty payment of 500 MYR from the sucker - that too is decided by the management most of the time - especially for suckers who win over 100K & want to leave the next day then it's up to me to serve them in bed & make them stay so that they play more & loose..."

"Tch tch, that's not fair."

"I know - it's not fair on the part of management - the old casino on the other part of this complex is fair but they don't hire us..."

"You mean to say - there are 2 casinos in this complex?"

"Ya - this setup began about six months back after the owner died of sudden heart failure - that's strange because he was healthy & active - then his son made a deal with some business tycoon from China & leased a part for this casino."

"Hmm... interesting"

"I hate those bastards with whom I'm sent to sleep - most of the time - I decline - but I've a family to support in Thailand & sometimes they demand lot of money. Actually, we border around Thailand - to escape prostitution which is so very prevalent in Thai - I came here - but I feel that mostly all around the world - this is the truth - for every vulnerable woman..."

'How True' Chaits thought.

"Sometimes I wonder if I'll meet some good guy like you who has a will to look away from girls like me & be mine - I'll be glad to leave all this, even if he's poor."

Chaits was moved by her plight & put a comforting hand on her shoulder, "Keep wishing this in a positive manner and always - I mean always - believe in Him" he pointed at sky, "I'm sure you'll meet someone."

"Oh! That's so kind of you to comfort me like this..." she said wiping a tear ready to overflow.

She sipped her beer & controlled herself looked at Chaits & gave a wry smile, "So dumb of me" she said tapping her forehead, "here you're looking for entertainment as a tourist and I am putting a bucket of my personal woes in your lap."

"Oh! No - don't think this way - I'm in sales - that's my profession & I love to hear people talk - I like it the most when they bravely put forth the real words, emotions & feelings... Please go on - I swear - after you finish - you'll feel great..."

Her knee had stopped touching Chaits - there was no more a display of false coquetry - she was now - her own self - a lonely girl with plenty of true emotions in this big bad world...

"Would you like another beer?"

"No - it's alright - I want to get out of this revealing dress & be myself." she said with a sigh.

"Aw-right - then - Good Night" said Chaits, "and don't you forget to make that wish - true & from bottom of your heart - you'll realise your dream one day."

"Please don't go" she said pleading, "after a long time - I've met someone who's good at heart & is a human being - you're not like other wolves - lusty & frustrated - I already have started feeling better - after I started to talk to you..."

"But, Laila - you said, you wanted to change into normal clothes - so you must be going to the powder room - right?"

"Heck-no..." she said laughing, "we change our clothes in our quarters & we walk in these clothes all the way - who knows - we might lure in some sucker from the other casino to this one. I hope you don't mind accompanying me to my room - Chaits?"

He thought for a moment, 'Hell - I'm in Malaysia & nobody knows me here.'...

"Is that allowed?"

"Ya - in fact - if we have to take any suckers for the night, it's always done in our quarters - initially - we used to go to their rooms - but some bastards accused us of stealing their money after they lost at the casino - so the management redecorated our rooms & decided that all suckers need to go to our quarters."

'Oh! My word - these people seem to have solutions for everything' wondered Chaits as he walked with Laila... conscious to strange glances rendered by other people...

"Don't mind these glances" she said, "they are surprized because you're not holding me or touching me as the other bastards do."

"Oh-ok" he murmured.

They walked through the long corridors before they came to an exit - she pushed the door & they walked out of the main building, "This's the parking for 2-wheeters she said pointing to the right where lots of bikes were parked, "In fact, we've asked the management to shift this parking because when they exit the campus - they ride dangerously to tease us - it becomes difficult for us to cross over to our quarters..."

Chaits looked at a small 2-storeyed building they were approaching - it looked more like a hostel of a college in India.

"The stairs are here" she said pointing toward left as they entered - she crossed over & walked straight till they reached the elevator, "My room's on the first floor - right at the end" she said as they entered the elevator - they both were silent till she opened the door to her room 'Boy! Is this cosy?' Chaits thought as he scanned the spotless room

- decorated romantically...

"Please feel comfortable" she said and she disappeared in the bathroom. Chaits waited patiently for her to reappear. He looked blankly around at the furniture - his glance was arrested by the corner table that had two frames - he got up & lifted those - one contained a sweet looking girl in her early twenties & the other was what seemed like a poor peasant family...

"That's my family" he turned around to look at Laila wiping her face with a towel - her make up washed away - she put her towel on the chair & saw Chaits unable to take his eyes off her. Without her heavy make cup - Laila looked sweetly attractive - just like the other frame - she was still wearing her casino uniform but looked decently sexy "What are you looking at?"

"I was wondering - what is such a sweet looking girl doing here?"

"I told you - I'm a Lucky Charm Girl who occasionally is led to prostitution which I hate..."

"But then you said you're a choice to deny..."

"Not everyone - but I've an option. On my way here from the casino - I ask the bastard what he would prefer to drink - when he tells me his choice - I ask him to wait and go to the 24hr bar where my friend Han bartends - she mixes the drink & by the time he's ready to jump on me the boy gets the drink - after that - I allow him to touch me for few minutes - he passes out & I just lie beside him so that he feels he had sex with me...." They both laughed at her trick...

"So tell me about your family."

"As I said, I come from a poor peasant family at the border of Thailand - my elder sister was pushed into prostitution in her early teens & she's been supporting all of us - then I grew up. It was decided that I'll have to join her - but I know how much she hates being a branded prostitute - my father has a loan on his head & expected us to repay it - even he didn't like the idea - but there was no other option..." she said holding her tears back.

"If you don't mind - could you tell me how much is the loan?"

"Well, it's about 70K MYR - we've been able to repay about 50K - between me & my sister we've been able to collect about 10K more - "Oh! How I wish I had 10K more - we'd repay the entire loan & then there'd be no pressure on me or her to get into prostitution."

"Keep complete faith in HIM - I'm sure HE will help a good girl like you - I wish, I could help - but I don't know how much money I'll need for next few days - If I'm left with money before I return to India - I promise - I'll give that all to you."

"Oh! I didn't mean to ask you for money" she said her eyes wide, "I know - I'll have to be in this dirt for another year at least - after that I'll have enough money & I'll quit & go back to my family."

"I like helping good people - and I now know that you're a good girl - so I will help you."

She looked at the celling trying to control her feelings - but she could hold on no more - she sank on the edge of sofa & started to weep inconsolably - Chaits sat next to her of put a comforting hand on her shoulder - she turned around & flung her arms around him & wept her heart out - after sometime she controlled her feelings & got up - she disappeared into the bathroom again. Chaits could visibly see the change in her as she stepped out & starred dabbing her washed face with the towel - she looked quite relaxed & content - she put her towel away & smiled at him...

"Thank you - Chaits as you said - I feel much better - my faith in HIM is renewed - you've shown me that there are good people in this world - and I'm ready to put hard work so that I can return to my family - as soon as possible."

"Oh! That's nothing - I'm glad that I was of some help to you - do you have a number where I can reach you?"

"Ya - I've a mobile phone - but I can answer it only between 12PM & 4PM because I've to start my work at 5PM & I wake up at 12.00PM - I work till 2 or 3 AM" she gave him the number & he stored it in his mobile.

"Give me your mobile number - I'll call you the day I earn those 10K MYR & go back to my family."

"Here - this is my business card."

She took the card & kept it in her purse. She looked at him & smiled - he smiled back at her, "Oh! My God!" she almost screamed... "So silly of me - I've made your shirt go completely wet with my tears - please let me wash it for you."

"Oh! That's alright - it'll dry off within no time."

"Would you like to drink another beer?"

Chaits looked at her as she got up & walked over to the refrigerator - she brought out 2 cans of Heiniken - Chaits accepted & they sat sipping beer. Now that her tension was off - she looked all the more beautiful & attractively sexy - 'Control yourself'' Chaits kept on saying within - he got up a threw the empty can in the bin next to the bed & turned around causing a misbalance & landed on the soft water-bed.

"Why are you looking at me like that?" her question was that of a girl full of innocence - it seem the she had found her real-self... Chaits paused for a moment. His face developed a mischievous smile, "I was wondering if my beer was mixed."

"No!" her indignance was clear, "these were sealed cans - straight of out of the factory." she stopped as Chaits started laughing & realized he was pulling a fast one - she first laughed & then put on her girlish mock anger "Yoouuuu..." she screamed in mock anger & made a dash for him - the bed was deep enough to slow his movement - she couldn't control her momentum & fell over him - stunned by the impact - they got up - she found herself sitting on his lap - her arms around him - they looked at each other for a moment breathing each other's breath - their eyes locked... She slowly bent forward & kissed him...

"This is not right - Laila"

"This is perfectly right..." she said In a firm but sexy, husky voice, "listen Chaits, till now I've been able to avoid this by mixing drinks - but who knows - one of the suckers who comes here may be a teetotaller - which is rare - but a chance - in that case I may have to yield - and if I've to yield - I'll rather yield to you."

Chaits opened his mouth to say something but she was quick enough to seal it - with her kiss and she started unbuttoning his shirt, kissing him over. He could control it no longer - his hands artistically started exploring her curves & she started loving his tender touches - yearning for more... Chaits had no difficulty to bare her - she was still in her two-piece bikini dress.

"Now I know" she said gasping for breath between kisses & her ecstasy, "why people fall in love." she surrendered to Chaits' vigor & energy...

It was almost 7AM when Chaits kissed her bye & left for his room - they were supposed to assemble at 8AM for the breakfast & leave Genting at 10AM. He was feeling sleepy but decided to control till he boarded the bus - after that he could sleep till they reached their hotel in Kuala Lumpur.

He opened the door to his room & looked aghast - someone had been there in his absence & had opened his bag - all his clothes lay helter-skelter - scattered around - his hands first checked for the 5000 MYR in his pocket - they were still there - then he looked around & was glad to find his passport & other important documents - he remembered putting 20,000 MYR in his bag - sure that the burglar had taken the cash, he started gathering his clothes & put them back in the bag - he looked around to check if he'd missed on anything... his eyes fell on the wad of those 20K MYR which seemed to be hurled toward the door - the money was still intact - he gladly picked up the wad of put it in his bag...

'If the guy who broke into his room, was not looking for money - why was his room broken into - what was he looking for?' Chaits couldn't help thinking - he made sure that the door was locked & kept the bathroom door open and he freshened up for the day - got ready to travel & was in for the breakfast early - still brooding over the break-in...

"Hi... I'm Han" a girl introduced herself, smiling at him, "I'm Laila's friend - what did you do to her? I've never seen her so excited and happy before - I'm happy for her."

"Oh! I did nothing - she just realized her own-self. I'm happy for her as well - she's started believing in herself."

"What time are you leaving?" she asked as she deftly served him the breakfast, "she wants to meet you before you leave."

"Oh! Around 10AM" Chaits said munching on his breakfast.

"You don't seem to be so happy - do you mind if I ask why?"

Chaits related the break - into his room when he was with Laila...

"That's simply not possible - the rooms here are securely locked with electronic key combination."

"I know - but that's what's happened."

"I would suggest you complain."

"That'd make no sense... Nothing's stolen or missing - so what can I complain about?"

"That's strange..." she looked bewildered as she thought, "Excuse me - I got to serve other people - but please accept my thanks for making her feel so happy."

"Hey! Chaits!" that was Christy, "You seem to have enjoyed your night here at the casino - mine was bad - I lost 200 MYR - what about you?"

Chaits gave him a triumphant smile, "I won 25000 MYR"

"Ooohhh" that was reaction... "You are lucky."

Chaits smiled, "I had a Good Luck Charm."

"You..." Christy said knowingly, "you'll never change & your luck never seems to run out - whether it's money or the girls..."

They laughed & jested, Chaits had no mood to share the break-in.

"Guys - let's assemble - we got to move..." that was Sudhir...

They assembled with their respective baggage - everyone wanted to enjoy the ropeway again - so they put their bags in the bus & started toward the ropeway - Chaits couldn't help looking back one more time at the complex as they waited for their turn for the ropeway - they had lagged behind others & were the last in the queue - Chaits was happy to be the last in queue - they had started at 9:30 AM & he'd told Han that they'd be leaving at 10AM - he impatiently waited for Laila - she didn't arrive - it was almost 10.30AM when his turn came to board the ropeway - he was about to board when he heard a faint shout

"Chaits"

Christy & he turned around to see Laila run toward them, "Thank God!" she said between her inflated breath, "I found you" she looked at him & gave a sad, melancholy smile, "For all that you've done for me, Chaits" she said & hugged him - then kissed him - long & sweet, "I guess it's farewell then..." she said holding her tears which did overflow. She pulled out a golden locket studded in jade & inscribed in some oriental language & put it around his neck, "This is for you to remember me, to be your 'Good Luck Charm Girl' - ever... "

The ropeway started & she kept on waving & weeping till he could see her - no longer...

## CHAPTER TEN

Soon - they were seated in the bus & Chisty related the reason for their delay describing the latter part where Laila gifted a gold chain - adding each bit with a spice of his own...

Bhoopi Singh was all ears & his eyes were all wonder to Christy's narration "Don't tell me" Bhoopi was almost screaming - not ready to believe Christy's narration "you mean to say - this guy wins money - then gets to screw the sexiest babe in the casino - that too for Free - on top of that - the babe comes in running & gifts him a gold chain? - THIS IS SHEER - INJUSTICE"

"I'd love to learn the game of poker." Christy was enthusiastic.

"No great shakes - I will teach you..."

"But, I want to know the story after the casino" Bhoopi's hormones compelled him.

"Aw" said Chaits with a wave of his hand, "no great shakes about it - Christy can explain"

"I'd say it's better than great shakes" Christy said pushing an elbow at Chaits' & they laughed at his wit...

They arrived at the hotel in Kuala Lumpur - there was no specific plan for the day except the dinner with the MD of their organization - so Chaits made doubly sure that his room was securely locked & snored off to glory – a bit uncomfortable with crazy dreams but beautifully occupied by Lisha & Laila...

He woke up in time to get ready for the big dinner party - the MD of his company had flown in for this occasion - he was to give away the certificates of recognition & rewards for the top 5 achievers... and 2000USD to the best sales person - Chaits... The party went on after the rewards & awards ceremony - Chaits looked around & realized that his group is going to be on the booze for most of the night - he soon got bored & walked out of the party hall - he came back to the reception & sat down on one of the comfy sofas in the waiting room.

He asked for permission to smoke & lit up - he glanced around & saw a newspaper - for a long time, since he landed in this country - he had been out of touch with the world - he picked it up and started going through the news items - he was going through a news item related to a theft when he remembered - he'd to call the guy whose pouch & money was to be returned - he looked at his watch - 11:10 PM - this was no time to call a decent man - so he went back to his newspaper...

He looked up at the girl on the reception - like most of the girls - she had 'Impressed by him' look in her eyes as she smiled at him "How can I help you, Sir?" she asked

"If you can arrange for a tin or mug of beer - please..." Chaits said this in his special tone & a voice that normally made all girls go weak in their knees...

"Oh! Sure" she said and quickly & connected to the bar, "Would you pay or would you like it added to your room bill?"

"I'll pay." he said with a smile & started scanning the newspaper again - he looked up & paid as his beer was served - he was about to put the newspaper aside & turn on his charm at the girl at the reception when a news item caught his attention - he started reading it & was soon engrossed in this item... it was a follow up of a murder that happened on Sunday noon - it was a mystery... He glanced at the reception - the girl was still fascinated by him "Hey!" he said in his special tone again, "could you, please, get me the editions of this newspaper from Sunday onward?"

"Certainly" and she asked the bell boy to complete the task & gave a wider smile to Chaits...

He had the editions in next 5 minutes - he scanned the Sunday edition - no luck - he kept it aside - he started scanning Monday's edition - he found the item - he looked at the girl again, "Can I carry these back to my room?"

"Certainly Sir."

"Oh! That's very nice of you - thank you - by the way - I'm impressed by the service provided here - till what time are you here - I mean - what time does your duty end?"

"3AM, Sir" her voice quavered a bit...

"That's pretty late - and you go home after that?"

"Not always" she said, coy to his question almost suggesting she could stay on if he asked.

"Wow! Was nice chatting with you, see ya later..." he said with his typical boyish smile & made his way toward his room leaving the girl - her heart beating fast. Once the door to his room was securely locked, he changed into comfortable night dress & sat down with the newspapers...

'Sunday witnessed a mysterious murder of an unknown person in an empty flat. This happened in a remote suburb. One of the residents saw blood coming out of the door to a vacant flat & alerted police who swung into action.'

Chaits shook his head in wonder, 'and - I thought - such things happened only in India.'

'When the police forced the door open, they saw an unidentified man murdered in a ghastly style. The man was tied to a chair & tortured first. After that his neck was sliced & the head, separated from his body. The police have not been able to identify this man. Prima facie - he seems to be of Indian origin & may have travelled in from India or Pakistan. They cleaned & managed to give our reporter a photo of his severed head for identification - see page 10...'

He turned over the pages - he didn't want to read the news item any further - the photograph explained it all... He kept on looking at the face that was printed - it belonged to the passenger whose pouch full of money was with him... A chill ran down his spine – 'who could that person be - and why should he be murdered in this ghastly style - he seemed to be a good hearted, sophisticated person when I met him at the airport.'

Chaits kept on wondering, questions in his mind & a horrible photo in front of his eyes - he got up & opened a can of beer, lit up a smoke & closed his eyes - concentrating hard to clear his mind & put the pieces together in the order of events...

'Wait! - We started off Saturday night & boarded this flight early Sunday morning - Sunday morning we landed & accidently - his pouch remained with me - the same day around afternoon - this guy is murdered. That's when I realized, his pouch was with me. This clearly means that he'd travelled this for to pay this amount to the people who murdered him - poor chap - he was dead even before I realised that the pouch contained all this money. Who could've killed him? - Probably the loan sharks - I've seen this in lot of movies - people gamble - they take loans - then they are pressed money & get killed because they're unable to pay the loan - that must be it - there's a casino at Genting Highlands...'

Chaits woke up - a bit of hangover gripped him. He had been unable to sleep soundly after he'd read the newspaper & the guy's face haunted his dreams... He joined others at the breakfast Christy was quick to notice his silence & looked at him in wonder...

"Nothing" Chaits brushed him off - didn't want the entire group's mood to be tense "had overdrunk yesterday - a bit of hangover." That was an acceptable reason & Christy went back to his breakfast - they boarded their tour bus - to take a look at the modern city...

Chaits was in no mood to check the city out, his mind was still occupied by the murder of that co-passenger & he mechanically tagged along with his group... Late afternoon - they were back & Chaits realized - he'd seen nothing or remembered nothing of the day's tour...

"From now till we leave on Sunday evening, it's free time for you guys - you can roam where you want to shop - there are quite a few shopping places around - but I think you'd like to start with a couple like 'Globe Silk Store' which has decent rates and a Japanese venture called SOHO..." Sudhir announced.

The group freshened up & made their way toward the shopping centres, once there - Chaits stopped brooding & was excited - he checked the memos in his mobile phone - he had made a note to purchase mementos for lot of people - family & friends back there in India... The first thing he purchased was a convenient bag which could hold few minimum required clothes & which he could easily hang over his shoulders resting on his back - this was something he planned to carry along when he'd be travelling along with Lisha in the next week...

He then went over collecting mementos & checking the list in his mobile - the bag was reasonably filled up with choice items for everyone on the list... He was about to exit the mall when he glanced on an oriental dress - it was slimly stitched & looked great in its dark olive green colour it had a designer top & a flowing long skirt - he touched it - it was excitingly soft & smooth - the price tag showed 1500 MYR - but it was worth the cost - he decided to buy the dress - he'd gift that to someone special on a special day & he packed it - he exited from the complex & started walking toward the main road - he saw another shop next to it...

The shop was small in size was displaying a lot of locally made clothes - what had caught his interest was the 'Lucky Charm Girl' dress which reminded him of Laila & he folded his arms in prayer for her. He entered the shop & checked - these dresses were a craze at high society parties & the range started from 200 MYR... He shook his head sadly 'Will these high society women ever understand the woes of those girls who actually wear these as uniforms?' he thought...

He got a cab & returned to the hotel & started re-packing his bags - he didn't want to carry so many bags around when touring with Lisha. So he segregated - he kept all the mementoes in his big bag - he realised that his memory card in the mobile was full & he needed to move the contents into another memory device or buy new one tomorrow... He had almost finished his packing when he looked at the pouch again - clearly - the guy had nobody he knew in this country - else even they would've been killed - why else did he carry an address & a telephone number with him? - The cash is no good for a dead body - Chaits thought 'so what can I do with this cash? - Hey! - I got an idea - I'll give this cash to Laila - at least she'll be free from the predicament she's in... This money will be used for something good - that'll add to the guy's good deeds & hope that it'll take him to heaven...!'

He put the toiletries contained in the pouch in the trash can & pulled out the cash - he now knew how to use it - he rewrapped the cash & put it in the sack - he remembered the USB that was hidden in the pouch, 'Well - this sorts out my problem of transferring data - I don't need to buy another memory card at an exorbitant cost in foreign currency - I'll transfer all my photos in this USB'... satisfied at the way he'd segregated & packed, he locked the room & came up to the reception - the girl, the same girl was at the counter & her eyes showed more expression of want as Chaits approached.

"I have some work to do but I've forgotten to carry my laptop from India - do you have a pc where I can use my USB?"

"Yes - Sir - take a right from the bar, we have a business centre - you'll get a pc with internet there."

"Thanks" said Chaits leaving her with faster heartbeats as he smiled at her... he entered the centre & got hold of a pc - he was content as he sat with his back toward the wall giving a complete privacy to him & the screen of the pc from any prying eyes - he booted the pc ON & inserted the USB & - 'Hey!' he thought, 'let me see what it contains - I might get a clue to who he was & maybe some link to alert his people in Pakistan about his death...'

He explored the USB, he found folders - those folders had names of various cities in Asia 'I know', he thought, 'I'm wrong in trying to access data of someone else - but this'll at least help me to know who he is or for whom does he work. If I go to police with this info - they may think I killed the guy for his money as well, I'll have to handover all the money which I plan to give to Laila.'

He looked at folders that appeared in alphabetical order - Amsterdam, Baghdad, Bangalore, Bangkok, Delhi, Hong Kong, Islamabad, Kabul, Karachi, Kuala Lumpur, Lahore, London, Mumbai, New York, Rangoon, Seol, etc... '3 cities in Pakistan' - he could be from any place there. 'Mumbai - that's where I belong - and I know every nook & corner of this city - It'll be the easiest for me to approach his business friends there...'

He clicked on the folder - there were lots of numbers, coupled with odd numbers which didn't make sense. He clicked on one of them - it opened up a word file with a map of a busy business district with a huge red spot marking a busy square at the entrance of a business house, where lot of big business names operated - he knew the building. He had one of his major clients located there - yes - how could he forget Ms Christabelle who worked there - below that, was a list of weekdays & various times of days - of which 3 different times were highlighted. Chaits was not able to understand this data stored in the USB - he clicked on other files in the same folder & went through similar data showing various business places in Mumbai with highlighted days & time.

He was confused & clicked on other folders which had similar maps & data. 'Now' he thought, 'this is a strange data to store & carry around!' he was still not able to figure out why the data was stored, or what was its relevance...

'Wait - he travelled to Malaysia with me & was supposed to meet someone - instead that someone got him killed - if he was killed the day he arrived, who the hell spoke to me when I called? Were the people who answered my call his friends or his enemies?'

His chain of thoughts again made him unsettled 'and to think of it - every time I called - people came looking for my belongings - first in Penang - where they got beaten up by Mostafa's men - then my bag was ransacked after I called from Genting Highlands - hmm - that's the reason I was asked - how I look - what I wore & which room number... they were looking for this USB & not the money I carried - what does this data actually mean?'

He carefully started checking each and every file for anything that would enlighten him...

He was soon frustrated as each file contained a map, weekdays & highlighted times - nothing more... he finished scanning each file in each folder - the only difference was the location & highlighted times - he was tired at the mental work he had done for past two hours - he desperately wanted to smoke - he was about to put off when he got an idea - he entered the menu again & clicked on 'Show Hidden Files' - lo! There popped up 2 new files - named J1, J2 - one was an XL spread sheet & the other in word - he was tired of looking at the word files & opened the XL sheet...

'Final Plan to Heaven' that was the heading beneath which was a matrix of cities in columns & times in rows - the squares corresponding were filled with numbers - he found the numbers familiar – 'Oh! These are the file names that he had been reading - now this is making some sense' he thought, 'so these are the locations & these are the dates - but there are multiple times attached to each...'

He looked at what seemed like a quarterly schedule - but still didn't make any sense - he closed the XL & opened the word file - what he read, made his blood chill & he started sweating even in unreasonably cold AC of the business centre - it was a horrible plan to terrorise common people by the terrorists - the XL sheet showed the dates & locations planned for huge bomb blasts - across the world...

Chaits knew Mumbai well & if these blasts were huge - he put up a figure of over 100K people affected in Mumbai alone - he wiped the sweat off him... he had stumbled on something which was huge and dangerous...

'What should I do?' the question was too big for him to find an answer, 'should I approach the police here? - But then I don't know what level I should approach, the terrorists may even have informers lined up there - they don't know me & they don't know where I'm - till then this information is safe with me - I'm visiting the Indian Embassy tomorrow - maybe - I can meet the ambassador & tell him about this' he was all the more confused about this affair now 'I'll format this USB so that all the data is erased' he started the procedure but stopped short of confirming the action – 'this could be a copy of the main file - and - even if I destroy this data - the main file still exists - in fact - if I can hand this USB over to a proper authority - they'll be able to prevent these blasts - but who is the correct person?'

He removed the USB & put it in his pocket - he looked at the watch - almost 10PM. Tense - he walked out of the business centre & out of the hotel - still trying to figure out - his face suddenly lit up - his brother was worked with the Anti-terror Cell of Indian Army - he's the right person. He would know what to do with this information...

## CHAPTER ELEVEN

The main road was still busy though the traffic had dwindled. He saw a group of local boys & girls walking toward him, "Excuse me - Hi, I'm from India & I want to make an urgent call - could you please tell me where I can get a calling card?"

"At this time" one of them answered "you can find shops open in Little India - but it's far from here."

"Hey - thanks." he said & quickly checked & found a waiting cab, "Little India" he said as the taxi cruised along - most of the shops along the road were closed - as they entered the Little India - his hopes soared again as the shops still were open & in process of closing down for the day... He rushed out of the taxi & laboriously entered every shop till he found one - he bought a calling card of higher value & searched for a telephone booth...

"Hello" his mind relaxed when he heard his brother's voice, "Chaits" his brother seemed surprised at receiving his call from Malaysia, "do you realise that you're spending heavily on an International call?"

"Yes - but this is VERY IMPORTANT..."

"Something serious..." he could feel the tension in Chaits' voice - Chaits related his knowledge about the USB & how he came to possess it... "Now-listen carefully " his brother said in concerned but a firm comforting voice, "Do Not - I repeat - Do Not mention a word about this to anybody - keep the USB safely with you or at some safe place & get it back along with you - if you mention this to anyone else - they may find you & your life could be in danger - just behave normal & natural as if you don't know that the USB exists - I know - you're good at acting skills - treat this as a test of your acting skills & enjoy your tour - hand that USB to me personally on your return."

"OK"

"And, keep in touch - I'll see if I can arrange a protection for you through my counter parts in Malaysia - and - yes - Trust NO ONE..."

The card ran out of money & cut the call - Chaits felt a lot better after this conversation. He now had to keep that USB safe till he returned & hand it over to his brother... He hailed another cab & returned to the hotel...

"You look much better now." the girl at the reception said, "I was concerned when I saw you left, you looked as if you were sick."

"Oh! Thanks, for your concern - you're a lovely person" & he again left her with increased heartbeats.

Before going to sleep - he thought a lot about his find - he knew the USB, if he hands over to his brother would save at least 20 million lives as preventive measures could be taken. He was confident that he'd be able to pull off the act of ignorance - his concern was 'What if the terrorists find me before I return to India - there has to be a backup plan - I simply cannot hand this USB over to them & if they find me - I'm sure they'll kill me - irrespective - whether I give them the USB or not.' He made about 5 different plans & re-worked them.

The first thing he did after the breakfast was to go to the market & buy a memory card for his phone - after all - he wanted to capture every moment he spent with Lisha...

About noon they were ready for their visit to the Indian Embassy - he hoped that the extension of his visa would be denied...

Sudhir accompanied him to the embassy. They arrived at the embassy - Chaits put a chewing gum in his mouth to avoid any bad breath he may breathe due to excessive beer he had consumed the night before... After a brief wait, they were allowed to enter the embassy office - Sudhir helped him fill the legal forms & they had another brief wait. The officer on duty came back with a look of respect & looked at Chaits, "Col Khanna, security head of this embassy would like to meet you personally." He waived to a waiting guard to lead the way & asked Sudhir to wait...

Chaits again had a brief wait in his cabin & was awed by the heavy furniture - someone entered - he looked about 45 years in age, was hefty & well built - he looked what he was - a tough soldier...

"Hi - I'm Col. Khanna" he introduced and extended a warm hand toward Chaits.

"Hi - I'm Chaits, I mean Chaitanya."

"Good - I've been reading the application for extension of your visa as well the letter of recommendation from your company - you seem to be quite an achiever - and I like people who harness a zest to win."

"Thank you, sir."

"Oh! C'mon - you don't have to be so formal - you should be proud of your achievement - we have faxed your application to the authorities here, waiting for them to revert - should not be a problem - how do you like to be here?"

"Oh! It's a wonderful country; much like India - you've diverse cultures merged & the local people are very helpful & friendly"

"Any adventures?" Col Khanna asked.

"Oh! Not much! Just the water sports - I enjoyed them at Penang."

"Good! - I think they'll extend your visa for 3 months - how long do you plan to stay?"

"To tell you the truth - I'll love to return with my group."

"Why?"

"It was fun when they were around - I'll be lonely if I stay back."

"Now-now - my son - feeling homesick already - you seem to be a friendly person - I know that... I've been a good judge of people - I'm sure, you may've made some friends here..."

"Ya - I did - but we can always be friends over internet as well - I really do wish to go back with my friends & colleagues."

"That seems a bit difficult..."

"Why?"

"You have ticket for next Sunday & I checked - all the flights going to India or via India are full - that's the reason, I'm here talking to you. Don't think that you're alone here you can simply walk in or call me if you feel that you're lonely or if you feel that you're in some sort of danger - here - take my card."

Chaits took the card & carefully noted his number - all his hopes of returning to India were dashed - he'll be sure not to miss the fight next Sunday.

"And yes, before you return, we'll have another round of chat in this room - you'll not be allowed to leave this country without my approval & regulatory stamp."

"Ok" Chaits nodded," but what if they deny the extension of visa?"

"Oh! Don't worry about it - we'll accommodate you in one of our cosy guest rooms here till we secure a flight for you." he said smiling. Someone knocked on the door.

"Excuse me, Chaits, I'll be back in few minutes - by the time enjoy sipping this hot coffee..."

Chaits was tense again - one week to go - he had to keep the USB safe & evade the terrorists... His hands groped below Col Khanna's table and he stuck the gum he was chewing, there...

Col Khanna returned with a broad smile even as Chaits sipped at the coffee "I knew it." he said jubilant, "they'll never decline my request - your visa has been extended by three months."

Chaits' heart sank - he was hoping that his visa would be denied & he'd be put up in safety of the Embassy - now - he'd be out & vulnerable - twice they had managed to find him - once at Penang & once at Genting Highlands resort - though, that was when he'd called to return the pouch - they may not remember him - he hoped...

He put up a smile, "Hey! Thanks..."

"You're always welcome, son, remember to call me if you get into trouble & meet me before you go" Chaits made an exit - a bit frustrated - this was one of those rare times when he had made a desperate wish that destiny had not granted. With heavy heart - he returned to the hotel - once in the room, he thought of Lisha elated his mood... The evening again saw a shopping mood of the group - Chaits had already packed & didn't want to shop but did want to see what was on offer.

"If you all are interested" said Sudhir, "visit an area known as Little India - you'll be able to experience the Saturday night bazar it starts around 8 PM & goes on till almost early morning."

The group was more interested in shopping around the famous Twin Towers - so Chaits decided to visit the night bazar it seemed hardly about 4-5kms from the hotel & he'd seen the way when he had picked up the calling card yesterday... So he packed his roller skates & put them in the small sack he normally hung over his back - he looked at the shopping around Twin Towers. It didn't interest him so much - he said bye to his group & hailed a taxi to Little India. The taxi stopped on the outskirts, "You'll have to walk from here, Sir" the driver informed, "they close the road for the bazar."

'Well, if the road has to be closed, then the bazar must be a big affair' & he started on foot toward the main road in Little India. Sure enough, the bazar looked great with the buzz around. It was yet to start & people were putting up their stalls to display the items they wanted to sell - he ambled around aimless when he saw a restaurant run by 'Hare Rama Hare Krishna Mission'. To his amazement he saw a familiar face in the crowd - it was Sharon - one of his girlfriends in Mumbai - she worked for a software company "Chaits! " she screamed not ready to believe her eyes, "what the hell are you doing in Kal?"

"I earned my incentive trip here." he said proudly.

"Wow! That's great - how long have you been here?"

"I'm here since last Sunday - our group returns tomorrow."

"Oww - had you called me – we'd have been able to enjoy the way we do in Mumbai" she winked at him.

"We might - still..."

"You mean - tonight?" she looked at him, her eyes dreamy about their last date on the beach of Murud, their romantic walk within the ruins of Janjira fort topped with crazy burst of lusty emotions for each other...

"Not tonight - maybe later next week - I can try & make it next Saturday."

"You just said - your group's leaving tomorrow."

"Ya - I said my group - not me."

"Oh! Then why not tonight?" she said putting her arm around him - teasing him with soft touches.

"My boss is with me - he won't like the idea of me romancing someone from one of my major business accounts - once they leave - I'm alone here & that'd give us the chance."

"So what are your plans?"

"I'm planning to go back to Penang - I've a deal with a local guide there."

"A girl?"

"How do you know?"

"Your eyes are expressive Chaits, they don't lie, at least not to your girlfriends and least of all me. Your expressive eyes are the very reason I got attracted to you - I know - you've many girlfriends in Mumbai & I hate them - they are my competition - but - I love you - I know your friendly flirtations - you try to impress every girl that crosses your path - but you're different -you really feel for each girlfriend & you never take advantage - you are more like a crocodile - you'll wait till she's desperate to jump in bed with you I hate you..."

Chaits looked amused, 'My God! Why do girls have such complex method & thought process?'

"Hey! Listen..." he turned on his charm, as he spoke in his special soft voice, "don't overwork your brain - I'm here - right now - with you & I'm sure we can definitely enjoy a romantic walk in this bazar."

"I can kill you for this Chaits" she said in mock anger & lovingly put her arm across his waist & looked at him "I'm all yours."

They happily strolled looking at all the buzz around - hand in hand - close together. They shared a wonderful dinner... she showed him a tourism office where he booked an overnight bus to PENANG...

## CHAPTER TWELVE

Chaits returned to the hotel just in time to meet his group for breakfast - his heart was still beating fast - Sharon was in Kuala Lumpur on a project & was going to be here for another 3 months at least - after a wonderful dinner, he had gone to a simple accommodation she'd on rent in Little India - it was a cosy flat, though small - he planned to stay with her next Saturday. She had been lonely - so after she met him wanted him to stay for the night with him & had loved him like there was no tomorrow...

Chaits looked around & found Sudhir, "Can I ask you a favour?"

"Sure."

"I don't want to travel around with the heavy baggage - I see that you have a small bag - could you carry my bag along with you to India with the group?"

"Well - I could - but what about the customs people?"

"Oh! Don't worry - these bags contain my clothes & some mementoes - all within the prescribed limit - I'm sure - they'll not even bother you, please..."

"Ok" Sudhir said after a thought, "but what do I do with them?"

"Manoj or Christy can carry them back to Mumbai for me - I'm sure of that..."

"Then it's ok."

"Hey! Thanks for both - we had a wonderful tour here."

"My pleasure." he beamed.

Chaits requested Manoj to take care of his bags "No probs - Chaits - I'll keep them secure at our office - and if you wish I can arrange to deliver them to your home."

"Hey! You're my friend - I'd be delighted if you can deliver these to my home."

Chaits heaved a sigh of relief, now if he had to run from the terrorists - he was prepared - he would be travelling light - in such an event, he'll pay Lisha what he'd promised & run away from her & the terrorists - he'd ask Col Khanna to help him stay at the embassy till Sunday - he'll not put anybody else's life in danger along with him... But it will depend if the terrorists knew that he's the person who'd accidently received the USB - if they don't - he had all the time in the world to enjoy...

In the evening, he said bye to his group & made his way to the bus stand - content that he only had a sack containing few clothes & his roller skates with all the money tucked in... It was a luxurious bus & the seats were comfortable - one look at them, he knew that he'd get a sound sleep... he found his seat & tucked his bag into the overhead cabin & started dreaming about Lisha as soon as he settled...

"Excuse me" a voice disrupted his day dream, "I think you're occupying my seat."

"Oh! - sorry." he looked at the seating arrangement & shifted over to the next one... He looked at the person & remembered the European female who'd booked the bus & the hotel at the same tourism office in Little India - she was behind him in the queue & he'd dared only a fleeting glimpse of her - Sharon would've created a scene otherwise...

"That's alright..." she said & smiled at him "you alone?"

Chaits' heart sank – 'she must have a companion & may now request me to exchange the seat 'pity - I'd have loved to sit next to her.'

"Yes - I'm travelling alone"

"That's great - so am I..."

'Wow! What a perfect setting' thought Chaits, 'I never had a chance to check my charm on a European female - and here, this one drops - right in my lap...'

"Wow!" he said turning his charm & the special voice 'on' - "travelling alone - in a foreign country - you got courage." he smiled.

"Thanks for the compliment" she was taken in by Chaits' flattery, "I'm Cynthia" she said extending her hand.

"I'm Chaits"

"Are you from Malaysia?"

"No - I'm from India, what about you?"

"I'm from Austria"

"For an Austrian - your English is good"

"I studied at Oxford"

"Well - that explains it"

She laughed & they chatted for some time as the bus cruised on the expressway - Chaits kept the conversation light & spoke only about beautiful Malaysia - he clearly remembered his brother's instructions. After a while they were sleepy & Cynthia dozed off - Chaits couldn't help intently watching her close - like all Europeans - she had a fair skin, she had blond wavy hair that fell softly over her square shoulders - he'd noticed her green eyes when they spoke - they seemed curt & not dreamy like most of the girls he'd met though she had a nice smile - she had clipped hair falling over & above her eyes & almost had a manly face - her juicy lips were exceptional...

He glanced downward - her hands, though slim looked tough - she must have overworked at the gym' he thought - her breasts were a bit big & shapely. Chaits had to control his urge to ogle at them as they heaved up & down which with her breath - he sized her up to be almost his height - she looked familiar to someone he'd seen on the TV but couldn't remember - all in all - she looks more like the WWF woman is wrestler - he concluded before he dozed off - he had to catch up on his sleep that he'd missed when Sharon had burst out with all her ecstasy the night before...

He woke up as the bus lightly jumped over the speed breakers at the toll plaza - he looked at the familiar Penang Bridge - he looked at Cynthia - she was delicately clinging to his arm as she rested her sleepy head on his shoulder, her soft hair tickling his elbow "Hey! Wake up - we're almost there" he gently woke her up & she opened a green eye to him.

"How do you know?"

"See - there - that's the famous bridge of Penang - I've seen this on internet - many times."

"Oh! It's lovely" she said even as the bus approached the bridge to cross - Chaits was thrilled as he looked at the vast expanse of water below...

"Where are you put up?" she asked as they alighted from the bus

"Ferrenghi Beach Hotel" Chaits replied blindly & bit his lip - he'd forgotten his brother's instructions for a moment, "I booked it yesterday - along with this bus ticket."

"Oh! That's great she said excited, "even I'm booked in the same hotel."

"What a coincidence."

"Let's share a cab" she suggested. They shared a cab - Chaits deliberately insisted on paying for the cab & asked her to go ahead & check-in... at least - she won't get as many details about him when he checked in - sure enough - she'd checked in & gone off to her room when he reached the counter.

"Good Morning, Mr Chaits - nice to see you again..." It was Lin & she definitely seemed happy to see him again.

"Hi - Lin - nice to see your sweet smile again - I'd like the same room."

"It's all yours" she beamed at him, her eyes clearly showing her admiration for him - the first thing he did after freshening up was go out to the telephone booth & call Lisha...

"Hello" Chaits heart went along for a joy ride as soon as he heard her sweet voice...

"Hi - Lisha - I'm Chaits."

"Oh! Hi Chaits! How are you? You didn't call for a week - so I thought you'd forgotten..."

"I'm sorry - the tour was a bit – err – hectic - and I used to get some free time only late in the evening - I didn't want to disturb you during your daily show."

"Where are you?"

"I'm at Penang - same hotel - I just met Lin"

"I thought you'd forgotten. Someone called me for an assignment in Kal - so I'm in Kal..."

"Oh! No - I just travelled overnight from Kal to Penang - how long is your assignment?"

"I wish - I knew - I got a meeting today afternoon - I'll call you after the meeting or you call me tomorrow morning."

"Ow - I'm going to lose one day then."

"Don't worry - I'll make up for that - speak to you again - tcha tcha..." and she hung up.

Chaits felt lost - all his dreams he'd seen were shattered. He didn't wish to tour the same places again - alone - with Lisha, it'd be different... Dejected, he returned & caught up on his sleep which had eluded him since he found the contents in the USB... Somehow, he felt safe in this room & slept like a log - he woke up late afternoon - he felt a lot better & a lot energetic - but bored - he'd nothing much to do - so he decided to catch up on his gym - his fitness & his stamina - he worked himself out at gym - satisfied at his strength & then tried his stamina at the swimming pool - all the while he kept thinking that he's going to need both - his strength & his stamina if the terrorists caught up with him & hoped they didn't know where he was at the moment - *he was wrong...*

Satisfied with his trial, he was about to get out of the pool - when someone jumped in - with a huge splash - he just managed to get the water off his eyes - it was Cynthia... she teased him more by splashing water on him playfully - he had no other choice but respond with a similar playful attitude. After sometime, they were absolutely friendly with each other & decided to stroll out in the evening & return for dinner. They strolled on the beach & she showed signs of liking him and she walked closer - hand in hand... By the time they had dinner - she seemed to be an absolute gonner & laughed away at his wit...

It was time to retire for the night and as they entered the elevator - he realised that she was occupying the room next to him.

"Which room - yours or mine?" she asked as she gently put her arm around him in a bold proposition...

"Mine" he said absentmindedly...

'I was right about her size' he thought as she undressed & approached him – her body was manly - was taught with heavy exercise - she possessed immense physical strength that almost matched his own - she was almost his height - the muscles of her arms & legs flexed tough with every move she made - the only soft parts he could feel were her juicy lips & her big warm breasts - it was not love making - it was more of love wrestling - finally he got better of her as she settled down - responding to his rhythm.

'Whew! What an experience' Chaits thought as he woke up - a bit tired after his tough love experience with Cynthia - 'Loving a WWF wrestler is tough' he thought & laughed at the idea - he reached out but she was not there - she'd left when he was sleeping - he got out of the bed - his eyes opened wide when he saw his sack open - he quickly whisked through his items - they were intact with all his money...

"Did she open my bag & searched for something - was it the USB she was looking for - if so, then she's a part of the terrorist outfit - if not - did I leave it open? The items seem to be intact & so is the money the thought made him uncomfortable. He was all thought as he freshened up & was about to lock the room when the intercom buzzed...

"Hello?"

"Hi - Chaits - It's me - Lisha"

"Oh! Hi – Lisha - what's the news?"

"Pack your bag - I'm in Penang & will pick you up in an hour - I've made arrangement of our tour." and she hung up.

He carefully packed his bag & locked his room behind him - he had a strong urge to knock on Cynthia's room & say 'bye' to her as a courtesy - but he refrained - it was almost time for Lisha to arrive & he hated the idea of making her wait. He checked out of the hotel.

"See you in the evening" Lin said smiling, her eyes wide in excitement - Chaits was confused as to why she said so

- even as he checked out, Lisha drove a car in the curb at the entrance & waived excitedly at him - he looked at her & waived back & yet again found his heartbeats increase – 'Boy! Does she look gorgeous?'

As he neared her car, she got off & hugged him with warmth & happiness... "Where's your baggage?" she asked astonished at the lone sack he carried.

"This is the only baggage I've - all the rest of it - I sent back to India with my group."

"Oh! That's nice..." she didn't seem convinced at Chaits' explanation - but didn't say a word. He sat in the car next to her as they drove off... "This is our home in Penang - she said as she parked her car - we have 3 bedrooms - for me, for Lin & one for our guest - you" and she smiled.

"Oh! That's the reason Lin said that we'll meet again today" Chaits said.

"Ya - she knew that I'd be putting you up here - in this house – welcome in"

It was a cosy small house with a small hall containing a dining table - a small kitchen & 3 small bedrooms but nicely furnished. "See - this is how I save your money."

"Wow - thanks a lot" Chaits' joy knew no bounds - he'd have Lisha's company - 24hrs - everyday of this tour.

As discussed, they started their sight-seeing tour around Penang & Chaits happily clicked away, his mobile phone camera capturing memories of Lisha...

## CHAPTER THIRTEEN

"Hi - Dinner's ready - I hope it tastes good - I'm not a wonderful cook" Lin said serving them with a smile - her eyes clearly showing her attraction for Chaits... Chaits tasted & praised her cooking ability - the food sure tasted tasty.

"Mr Chaits..."

"You can simply call me - Chaits."

"Oh - ok - Chaits - how long do you know Ms Cynthia?"

Chaits gulped the morsel he was chewing "Not much except that she was my co-passenger when I travelled from Kal to Penang & then she joined me for the evening walk on the beach & then she shared the dinner table with me - that's it - why?"

"It seems strange - she came running after you when you left with Lisha - she walked up to my counter and started asking questions to see if I knew where you'd gone..." Chaits gulped a glass of water, "she said she'd have loved to tour around with you share the expense."

"Oh! No..." Lisha said, "I will certainly not deal with two different clients at the same time & we don't have additional bedroom for an additional person..."

Chaits could sense jealousy ... "Did you tell her anything?" Chaits asked her.

"Oh - no - I'm smart you see - I told her that you had a deal with some tourism company & they'd made your tour arrangement - she was a strange female - she looked desperate to know about you & when she thought I knew nothing - she banged her fist hard on my table breaking the glass - then she called someone from her mobile - she paid up for the damage & 4 days of her booking & checked out with some mean looking men - they were 3 of them."

Chaits gulped another glass of water - his worst fears seemed to be coming true - 'was she a part of the terrorist outfit? Do they know who I am & where I am? - are they on a hunt for me? - or is this just a co-incidence' so many questions rushed through his mind in a split of a second, maybe - I'm dreaming & this nightmare will end when I wake up - and if this is not a dream - then and I'm putting both these sweet, beautiful girls in hell of danger...' He decided to wait for a couple of days to check if there was danger - he'd pay up for Lisha's service - call up Col Khanna & seek his help...

It was a bit tough for him to get a sound sleep - he was not accustomed to the local food and the thought of Cynthia being a part of the terrorist outfit haunted him... He woke up a bit late and was a bit concerned to find himself alone in the house - he chewed on the breakfast that was kept on the dining table with a note from Lisha, 'I'll be back shortly...'

He patiently waited for her return - he sat down & concentrated - trying to put together the sequence of what was happening - after some thought, he was ready to hit the panic button - he was almost sure that the terrorists knew the USB was with him & had identified him - now they were in search of him - he also knew that even if he hands the USB to them - they'd still kill him & whoever accompanied him.

'What should I do?' he contemplated but couldn't work out any specific plan - all he could do was feel unsecure & more worse - felt remorse that he was dragging Lisha along with him - his train of thoughts halted as he heard Lisha park her car...

"Good morning, Chaits" she said smiling as she entered, "I'm sorry - I'd to go out - Lin was had a flight to go to Cebu - she's going back home for few days."

'Oh! Good! So I'm alone with Lisha - one person less in danger" he thought... She looked at him & started singing 'Chiquitita' in a soft voice - Chaits looked at her and smiled sheepishly...

"You started brooding again?" she asked him & smiled.

"It's not what you think Lisha - and for your information – Chiquitita means a little girl..."

"I don't care what it means - for me, you are my Chiquitita and tell me about why are you brooding again - am I not your friend? You should always share your worries & your happiness with a friend" she sat next to him & put her soft comforting hand on his shoulder...

"Lisha" he started off in a serious tone, "I think - my life is in danger..." she looked at him with innocent eyes - as wide open as they could widen... "I was thinking about incidences that have occurred since I set foot in Malaysia - you remember the fight we had on the beach? - I think - that was not a coincidence - those people had come for me & you got into danger - unknowingly - solely because - you were with me."

"Do you mean - you were expecting that attack?"

"No - I thought that it was a coincidence as well - but - my room was broken into & my bags checked thoroughly by someone - when I was away - not once - but twice..."

"Hmm..." she said thoughtfully, "that could've been a coincidence as well - tell me how do you know that it was done deliberate."

Chaits related the story of how he got a pouch accidently at Subang Airport - how he tried to contact the person during his last visit to Penang - pointed out that they were attacked later...

"I see - but what was in that pouch?"

"Except cash of 50K MYR - it was full of toiletries like his shaving kit, etc." he deliberately omitted mention of USB from the list, "I know how much hard work you need to put to earn so much money - so as an honest person - I tried to contact him to return his money..."

"Then those people must have known about the money & must have attacked you for that..."

"I hope & wish - it was true."

"Why do say that?"

Then he related how he'd won money at Genting Highlands casino - how he'd kept the money secure in the room & how he'd met Laila & given her a hope to live - how she had thanked him by gifting him a gold pendant - he omitted the sudden rush of those intimate feelings when he was with Laila - Lisha was listening intently & stifled her position a bit when he mentioned Laila & being alone with her in her room...

"What happened then?" she asked... He told her how his room was broken into - how everything lay scattered around...

"Oh! My! They must have stolen all the money you had..."

"That's why I think I'm in danger - the money was untouched - I still am carrying the entire amount with me. You see - whoever it is - they don't want the money -

they're looking for something else."

"It must be something hidden in the pouch" she deduced logically, "can you show me the pouch?"

"Well - I don't have it anymore" he said truthfully, "I threw it in the dust bin at the Kal hotel" which he had indeed.

"Oh!" she said thinking about the experience he had "that's really strange - you shouldn't have thrown away the pouch - I'm sure it must have contained what they were looking for..."

"Now that you say - I think you're right - it must have contained something - but what?" she didn't have any answer to that question "so - you see - they don't know that I threw the pouch in a dust bin & they think that I still possess it"

"Are you keeping some info from me?"

Chaits was confused himself & thought hard, "Oh!" he almost screamed as he remembered, "I forgot the most important part."

"What?"

"Remember - I arrived last Sunday - that's the day we met first time..."

"Um-hmmm"

"The guy who owned the pouch was on the same plane & he was murdered the same afternoon."

"What?" she asked a bit stunned.

"Wait" he said & got up - he came back with the newspaper, "there - read it for yourself..."

She quickly went through the news item and looked at Chaits - she got up & hugged Chaits in concern, "You should have informed the police - it's still not late - we can go to them – today."

"I did think that I should go to them - but what else will I tell them - they'll think that I killed him or got him killed for all that money & am now making up a story to avoid arrest."

"Oh! I didn't think this way - you're right - they can arrest you for his murder."

"So I decided to keep quiet about the whole affair - quietly slip away from Kal & join you here at Penang & hope that they'll think I returned to India with my group."

"That was smart thinking" she smiled "they'll not know where you are - you're with me..."

"That worries me more - especially - about your safety."

"Why?"

"You remember Lin mention Cynthia?

"Yes - I do" she said a bit annoyed at the mention of her name - she wrinkled her nose in disgust, "what about her?"

"Now that I think - she was standing behind me when I booked the bus to Penang & the hotel room - she was in the bus - sitting next to me, outright friendly from the moment she settled down - she was booked in the same hotel in a room that was next to mine - and when I woke up in the morning - my sack was open - I'm sure - I'd shut it ... again no money is missing - I thought I must have left it open - but now when I think about her behaviour with Lin - I've my doubts about her..."

"Hmm - seems your thinking is right."

"So - Lisha - I think I'll have to say SORRY to you - pay you the amount I promised for your services as a tour guide & go off - I simply cannot put your life in danger."

"Are you crazy?" she asked angrily "If you go out there - you'll be found by them in no time - they're familiar with the geography & language - you're not - you'll easily be the odd man out..." Chaits saw logic in what she said, "I know each & every part of Malaysia & I can hide you till you're ready to return - further - whatever you're thinking could be wrong - I'll confess that you're very impressive & you easily attract girls - maybe Cynthia was impressed by you & wanted to stay with you in that case - this is just your imagination..."

"Lisha - I wish - what you say is true - but - if I'm correct in what I think, your life will be in danger along with mine & I don't want that."

"Shut your mouth" she said putting her hand gently over his lips, "if we're friends - we'll be friends forever - and if you've to die - I'll die before you..." Chaits looked at her serious expression not knowing what to do or say - Finally - he yielded. "Good" she said & entered her bedroom leaving Chaits to recover his normal self - she came back with a sack similar in size that Chaits had - "just in case - if you're right - we may not be able to return home - pick your bag - let's go..."

They locked the house behind them "Be a happy tourist - you can be gloomy if we really are in danger - c'mon..." she said & tickled him... he laughed at that & put his misery away - he looked at the brighter side - Lisha!!

## CHAPTER FOURTEEN

"By the way where are we going?"

"After what you told me - we're first going to the Kek Lok Si Temple - I'm going to pray for your safety - I know - my prayers are always heard by Buddha - he blesses me and grants my wishes."

"Nice idea - I'll pray for your safety - now that I know you're going to be by my side every moment - I don't want any trouble for you."

She laughed "Would you like to listen to some music?"

"Why not? I love music - I'd like to listen to some oriental music - if you have any collection with you…"

"I have" and she put on a CD - Chaits was concentrating on the notes, the tones of the silent rhythm of the instruments used "I think - you're bored - let me play some English songs" she said after a couple of tracks.

"If it's English songs - I'd prefer you singing them in your sweet voice."

She laughed, "I can either sing or I can drive - what'd you prefer?"

"You drive" he said grinning at her. Soon they approached a hill & Lisha stopped at a junction.

"There are two routes - one that I always take - it's a bit of hard work. You need to climb stairs - that way you pass the Liberation pool - after which you can enter the temple - the other easy way for lazy bums is to drive uphill through the curvy road & waste precious fuel - what would you prefer?"

"I'm not a lazy bum - I will take your way - maybe - Buddha blesses you because you prefer the hard way to reach HIM."

"Ok" she said & pulled the car to the side & parked, "there's a parking about a kilometre from here - but the road is small & the parking is normally full - this is the largest Buddhist temple in entire south-east Asia and lot of pilgrims visit here."

"Oh! Should be quite an impressive structure." said Chaits as he got out of the car.

"What are you carrying?" she asked

"These are my roller skates - I always carry them - if I get bored of walking - I skate"

"How will you skate on the stairs?"

"Simple - I'll take the road - downhill - that'll also give me some exercise" she waived her head in wonder...

It was reasonably hot & the walk to the base was tiring & the climb was tedious. But, as soon as they reached the Liberation pond - Chaits found a surge of energy sprouting within – 'Hmm - India is not the only place where you experience such a mystical magic - which proves - GOD is everywhere.' he thought.

"Lisha! Stand there - I want to click a photograph" she obliged putting her best smile - they climbed on - Chaits looked at the huge complex consisting of many buildings & caves - it was a magnificent sight...

"Let's first go by that inclined lift uphill - we'll first take the blessings of Kuan Yin."

"Who is he?"

"It's she - SHE is the Goddess of Mercy - SHE will bless our souls & wash away - any sins we may have committed."

Chaits thought of all the sins that he may have committed - including enjoying the passionate explosions of the girls he'd impressed - then about the sins - he was yet to commit - trying to save himself & the dangerous data of terrorism he had stumbled upon - 'I definitely need to wash away all the sins - that way, I might be able to succeed in getting the data intact to my brother & save lots of innocent lives.'

The inclined lift led them to a magnanimous statue of Kuan Yin and they both bowed with respect to get their souls cleaned - Chaits was fascinated by a pond there it seemed to be full of colourful fish, "These fish are known as Koi" Lisha explained, "Gold fish evolved from these..."

They made their way back to the Temple - it was beautiful & serene - there was something in the atmosphere that put his mind at peace & gave him the confidence - come what may - he will win & the terrorists will lose - he looked at Lisha - she stood straight & still - her eyes closed, her hands folded in prayer - her concentration to her prayer was complete. He couldn't stop himself - he clicked a photo of her as she intently prayed - a monk approached & signalled - No Photography - Chaits looked at him & acknowledged. He sat down & folded his legs, then straightened his arms that rested on his folded knees in classic Yoga posture - he closed his eyes after concentrating on the main idol of Buddha - soon he was lost in trance - he felt the reception of Holy energy emanating from Buddha that surged through his veins - the experience was blissful & his belief of Good winning over Bad grew manifold - now his confidence turned into belief... He was bound to win this against the terrorists - his own life was not a concern - he prayed for those innocent people who'd die - if he failed...

He opened his eyes feeling better & thanked Lord Buddha for blessing him - he looked around but couldn't see Lisha - he searched for her but couldn't see her around inside the Temple - so he walked out & decided to wait for her near the stairs - she was already standing there waiting for him, "How do you feel now" she asked...

"Never so my life - I've felt so good."

"See - that's why I brought you here - any idea how much time passed when you were lost in your meditation?"

"Um-No"

"You meditated - more than 2 hours!!"

"Did I? I'm sorry - I made you wait so long."

"Forget it" she said with a smile, "I'm happy that you smile again - you look more confident - I'm sure Buddha heard my prayer & blessed you."

Chaits felt a bit of remorse - he'd prayed for all those innocent lives & had forgotten to pray for her safety - he turned back...

"Now what?"

"I forgot something - I'll be back in a moment" he rushed back & prayed for Lisha's safety.

"Shall we return?" she asked.

"No - I'd like to climb that hill and get a panoramic view of this temple - it's not only beautiful - it's Devine."

She laughed & they tediously trekked uphill for the view that Chaits wanted - they came to a level where he stood & looked amazed at the grandeur of the temple & clicked the vision and then her standing with the temple in the background.

"Why are you clicking my photos?"

"I want to cherish every moment I spend with you. After few days - I'll have to return to India - I don't want to forget how you look - because - time may make me forget your face - but I'll remember you as someone who made friends with me & stood by me staunchly, when I felt I was in danger of losing my life..." he knelt down, held her hand & softy kissed it "Thank you, Lisha"

Lisha was dumb struck by his display of emotions & moved by his sincere gratitude & took a step toward him & hugged him.

"I'll never forget you, Chaits" you she said overwhelmed, "you'll always stay in my heart."

He stood by her side & looked at the grandeur of the temple again when he heard a noise - it seemed like a bus on a slope - he looked around - to his amazement - a bus did pass them crawling up the hill. There was uphill a road about 50 metres away "Where does this road lead?"

"Back to where we parked our car..."

"C'mon - let's check it out." They climbed up to the road & stood there for a while to catch up on their breath. The view from there was magnificent.

"Chaits" Lisha called him even as he clicked another photo of her with the magnificent view as background "I don't mind, you clicking as many photos of me as you like - but promise me - you'll never upload them on any internet site nor will you share them with any of your friends."

"I promise."

"Hungry?" she asked and took the sack off her back - like a magician who gets a hare out of a hat - she brought out a pack of sandwiches & a bottle of water - they sat on the stone compound splashing their legs into the air - happily munching... They sat there for about an hour - just because Chaits was in love of the view of the valley & the temple that glowed...

"C'mon – Chaits - we need to trek - all the way down & then walk to our car." she urged & got up.

"How about we walking all the way on this road till we reach our car?"

"That's silly - it's very long this way" he was still sitting - they heard a car climbing the slope... I wish - I'd got the car here."

"Oh! C'mon - Lisha - let's walk..."

They looked at the cars - there were two of them - one behind the other. The people looked at them as they passed & then at the view behind them - the cars screeched to a halt as people got down - "Hey! Look at that..." one of them screamed in joy - Chaits looked in wonder as the cars left them & moved on...

"What are you looking at?" one of them asked the other.

"I think - this spot is perfect." they spoke in Urdu & Chaits understood that language...

"Let's wait for our cars to turn & come back - they should be here any minute" sure enough the cars returned & screeched to a halt again - the group behind started laughing which alerted Chaits - he sensed that something was wrong 'If we run downhill - these people can follow us & it'll be tough to lose them - what should I do? - I cannot put Lisha's life in danger - no way. I'll have to protect her' he judged about 9 guys standing out of the cars & 2 more on the driver seats...

"Chaits!" Lisha's scream alerted him more... "These people have guns" ... a fight would be suicidal...

"Get up - you two - and stand by the stone fence you're sitting on..." one of them said in broken English.

Chaits lifted his legs & made a U-turn - still sitting so as to face them - they indeed possessed guns & were pointing them at Chaits - as soon as they saw Chaits turn and struggle to stand up - they started laughing - he had managed to put on his roller skates in the meantime...

"Well, well - what do we have here - a guy learning to skate in the hills?" and they laughed again.

"This makes our job easier" another added, "we can simply throw them off the cliff - it'll seem like an accident - so police will not look for their killers" he then looked at Chaits, "where's the pouch?"

"What pouch?" Chaits asked feigning innocence.

"Don't look so stupid - the pouch you got at Subang airport - the pouch you wanted to return."

"I threw it in the dustbin - it contained things like toothbrush, toothpaste, etc."

"You're lying" he screamed.

"I'm not." Chaits insisted.

"Why did you throw it away?"

"When I got back to Kal - I read the news of the poor guy's murder & recognised his photo - if he is dead - who was I going to return those silly toiletries?" Chaits was deliberately extending the conversation - he was thinking hard to see how they could escape - no matter what - those terrorists were going to kill them - he understood that they may be safe till they find the USB they were looking for...

"Why did you put on your skates" Lisha whispered, "we could've tried running back to the temple - and then to our car."

"Do you think - we could have been faster than their bullets?"

"No"

"So - let me handle this - my way... I am a poker guy."

"Let me put a bullet through them..." one of them said impatiently.

"No - you idiot - we first need to get the USB from him & killing will not help - we don't want to alert the police here about our existence."

"What should we do?"

"Pack them in the car - let's take them to our base - I'm sure our ways of torture will make him speak like a parrot."

They were about to cross the road when everyone heard an approaching bus as it climbed the slope "Lisha" Chaits muttered between his teeth and she looked at him - one eye on the men across the narrow road "have you ever seen a baby monkey cling to an adult when the adult jumps one branch to other?"

"Ya - I've - what about it?"

"When I say - you become the baby monkey & cling on to me - be sure that your legs hold me by my waist - not below them..."

"What are you planning to do?"

Chaits saw the bus approach from the curve, the men hid the guns behind their back "Don't try anything stupid" they warned as the bus approached...

"Now - Lisha - now..." Chaits screamed and bewildered, she obeyed him - she jumped up & held him tight - Chaits took cover behind the slow turning bus & started skating downhill - carrying Lisha who clung on, the way he described - like a baby monkey. The men realised this too late even as some of them ran toward the curve where Chaits & Lisha disappeared while others scrambled back to their cars "stop them" they shouted...

The slope helped Chaits in picking up speed - the speed was fearful as they he approached the second curve...

"Chaits! This is dangerous! "Lisha screamed in his ear.

"Do you have a better escape plan?" he screamed back as he negotiated the second turn at high speed.

"No" she screamed

"Then - HANG ON" he negotiated the third turn & she kept clinging on - hanging for her dear life. Thanks to the slope they were going at hazardous speed now...

"Chaits!" she screamed again.

"What?"

"They're following us in their cars - they're shooting at us. They are coming closer..."

"Good - I didn't have a rear view mirror - keep yelling their position to me."

"One of them is very near - 50ft - they're gaining on us - 40ft - now 30ft - 20 - 10 - oh! my god!" she screamed as Chaits took a very sharp turn & she lost the sight of the car & stared at a deep valley - then she saw the car - uncontrollable as it dashed against the fence breaking it & flew down taking all its passengers to a gloomy death...

"That was great" she screamed in joy, "the car's fallen into the valley - one more to go..." now she had confidence on his skating skills & started enjoying the chase - the crash of the first car had slowed down the latter for a moment, which allowed them to gain comfortable distance away from them due to the curves on the road - they were not within shooting sight... Chaits had negotiated a couple of more turns when Lisha screamed again "I see the second one - it's about a curve behind - now I see it again - 70ft - 60ft - It's disappeared again - oh! My God! - 30ft - it's gaining on us... Chaits we've almost reached the base of this hill. You now have a straight slope for a distance till you reach a curve which is almost 90° to your left & then one last curve before the road straightens up and you reach plain road - you'll have to do something before that else the speed will be a problem."

"Thanks - how far is the car?"

"I see it approaching about 100ft"

Chaits negotiated a turn - sure enough - there was a straight road, almost about 500mtrs stretch & sloping downward - he knew he had to make most of the speed here - so he pushed on with all his strength - the slope definitely helped him & almost a straight patch made it easy - his eyes concentrated on every details of the road while his ears were all to Lisha who was screaming out the latest distance between them & the car - he judged the sharp turn was about 30ft away and the car following them about 10ft away & gaining on them - fast - his heart sank as he heard another car toot a horn - it was somewhere near the dangerous 90° turn - he felt trapped - if he takes the turn - they'd surely bump into the car & meet with an accident & be captured alive - if he tried controlling his speed - the second car was almost touching him - it would run them over - he desperately looked at the turn hoping for some solution...

It was a split second decision "Lisha - hold tight - don't let go whatever happens" he screamed & Lisha obeyed by holding on with all her might. He veered off to the wrong side of the road & kept on a straight path - hurtling at a great speed toward the fence - a huge signboard showed a sharp turn ahead - the car was almost touching him now - about 5ft behind - he extended his arm & grabbed the pole that supported a huge signboard even as the climbing car neared dangerously evading him - he could see the expression of surprise & fear on the driver's face as they dangerously evaded the approaching car by a whisker - his speed converted into a centrifugal force as he grabbed the pole & the force lifted him off his feet along with Lisha as they circled the pole - missing the car that followed them by almost a centimetre - the driver was already thoughtless & dashed on the side runner, uncontrolled, flying off the road & landing head first in a deep ditch...

Chaits somehow controlled their spin & landed on the ground & stopped - a dazed Lisha climbed down & they both looked at the crashed car below…

"You idiot!" the driver of the car they nearly had bumped into came yelling at them - they turned around - he looked as if he had a heart-attack.

"Sorry" Chaits gasped, "That car's brakes failed - we were just trying to save ourselves…"

The guy clearly didn't understand a word that Chaits said as he looked horrified at them - Lisha explained in the local language - and then looked at Chaits' horrified expression as he pointed something behind - the guy turned around & saw his car beginning to move backwards - he'd forgotten the hand brake - he raised a cry of alarm & ran behind the car - somehow, he dangerously managed to get into the car & stop it - he showed a fist at them - looked at the sky - he sped off away from them. They laughed their heart out - relieved that they were safe & unharmed.

"You did it - Chaits" she screamed in joy & hugged him tight & pecked him on his cheek "how do you plan to get to our car - it's almost 5kms from here…"

"You enjoyed a baby monkey ride - now enjoy a piggy back ride" he suggested laughing.

"Why not?" she laughed & clung to his back - he started on the slope again - gaining fearsome momentum - the speed now thrilled Lisha & she enjoyed the piggy back ride - waving gaily at the people who looked at them in disbelief - all along the way… soon they reached the car and sped toward Penang…

## CHAPTER FIFTEEN

Chaits saw familiar landscape as they neared Penang - she stopped on the way at Penang for filling gas "Chaits! Sorry to ask you - but you'll have to lend me some money."

Chaits reached out for his sack that lay on the backseat, "Will 5000 MYR be enough?"

She smiled, "I only need about 500."

"Keep these 5000 - we may need them" she took the money & tucked it in her purse.

"Full Tank" she told the guy who was filling in the fuel at the station - once done - she revved up the engine & they started their drive...

"Hey! Isn't your home that way?"

"We're going to Kal - I'm going to put you on the first flight available - back to India."

"Hmm - I was really considering that - but, then - why take the trouble of driving all the way to KAL – you can put me on a bus..."

"You are not a local & you don't understand the local language - you stand out even on a crowded road - you're in danger..."

"I know that..."

"Back there - when we sat looking at the temple when did you notice those men as dangerous - before they brought out their guns?"

"Lisha - one request - please speak slowly & in short sentences - I'm sorry - but it's difficult to understand."

"Oh! Sorry - I was asking - when did you realize that we were in danger?"

"It was when they started laughing."

"They spoke in foreign language."

"They spoke in Urdu - a language spoken in Pakistan & by some percentage of people in India - I do understand it but can't read or write."

"Oh! That explains why you put on your skates - you understood what they said..."

"Yes"

"If they spoke in local language, or may be Thai, Filipino, Korean or Mandarin?"

"I won't know the difference."

"I know these languages - perfect - and that's why - I want to come with you & see you take off to safety." Chaits knew this argument will go nowhere - so he kept quiet & let her drive... "Further she continued, I know each & every road that leads into KAL - as well - all the internal roads of KAL - that way I can choose a safe road when in danger - do you think they'd allow you to simply come into KAL & fly off without causing trouble?"

'Hmm - now this is one aspect I had not thought about' he tried convincing himself for Lisha to be with him - but deep down - he knew - he was putting her life in danger along with him... The drive was smooth on the expressway - except for the toll booths - it was already dark & the road seemed like & 2 blobs racing ahead of them...

Chaits looked at a small glass container - it was placed on the dash board of her car - colourful LEDs lit up in a sequence & created reflections of various colours as they fell on huge glass marbles that were placed within - he couldn't stop himself & tried lifting the top - it came off easily - he picked up a marble - it was huge - almost a size of a lemon & was heavy & hard - one could easily use it as a paper weight - he placed it back & looked at various tints emanating from it...

"Hungry?" Lisha broke the silence.

"Yes"

She pulled up at a food plaza "Hey! C'mon" she said, Chaits tried getting out of the car, but his legs were all cramped up due to the hazardous skating - he wondered how he had managed to skate on the slope carrying Lisha along with him - now his body - especially his legs were sore... they refused to move - Lisha understood his plight & moved the car to Drive & Carry Off counter - after a short drive - she veered off the express way & drove into a distant town it was a small town & most of the shops were shut - it was past 10PM.

She drove around the town & reached a hotel - she checked them in & helped Chaits get into the room, then she got the bags - she asked the bell boy to get something while they munched on their dinner - after sometime - the bell boy delivered a pan of hot oil which looked coloured...

"Chaits! Remove your clothes - I want to put this mixture on your body. Ancient oriental medicine - in few hours - you'll be ready to skate again..."

She helped him remove his clothes & made him lie on the bed - she applied the oil on his body with expertise of a masseur & then gently started to massage his sore points - he felt so comfortable that he fell asleep - he woke up to the chirping of birds at dawn & looked around he saw her asleep on the sofa.

He got out of the bed & flexed his body - sure enough - all his pain was gone. He was ready to skate again - the way she said.

He looked at her - sound asleep and admired the sleeping beauty - her face was partially covered by her tresses & she looked astoundingly attractive - Chaits found his heartbeats accelerating as he looked at her - he controlled & entered the bathroom - he bathed in cold water to take away the heat of his feedings.

"Good morning" she smiled at him as he stepped out of the bathroom, "how are you now?"

"Hey! GREAT! You have magic in your hands - thank you." she looked satisfied at his progress & freshened up, "Ready to go?"

Once again - they made their way to the express way - at reasonable speed - they still had about 6 hrs drive to KAL...

"By the way - is this your car?"

"Ya - it cost me about 5K MYR & a 1000 more for the makeup..."

"Make up?"

"Ya - it's a second hand car - but I own it" she said proudly.

"You've maintained it well..." she smiled at Chaits' compliment...

"I will show you the speed if you are not afraid of it..."

Chaits braced up & showed a thumbs - up in readiness "That car - brown in colour it's been behind us since we hit the expressway - I'll show you how to lose it..." she said excited as Chaits looked into the rear view mirror & nodded. She sounded a whistle as she shifted gears & pushed the accelerator - within minutes, the brown car had vanished from the sight... "See" she said - Chaits looked at the speedometer in concern - she was driving almost to its capacity.

"That car's faster - must have a faster engine" Chaits said as he looked at the brown car on their tail "I think he'd like to race with you."

"Is that so ?" she asked quickly glancing into the rear view mirror - but soon realised that the other car was really faster than her car - it came on from behind on the wrong side - Chaits saw the guys sitting in - they were showing thumbs down to them - he looked at Lisha - she looked frustrated. The guys lowered the glass & waived him to do so... "Don't do that Chaits - I'll hate it if they jeer at me."

"C'mon - Lisha - it's a part of game you started - slow down when I start lowering the glass - they'll pass off..."

She eased off the pressure on the accelerator as Chaits slowly started lowering the window - his judgement was wrong - the other car slowed down it's pace to match with theirs - the guy on the back seat was yelling at them - Chaits couldn't understand a thing, "What's that joker yelling about?"

"They want us to stop the car they say something's sticking out of the boot behind..."

Chaits looked back - their sacks firmly sitting on the backseat "They must be pulling a fast one I haven't seen you open the boot."

"I haven't & there's nothing inside - idiots..." she cursed them.

"Lisha!" Chaits yelled.

"What?"

"Speed up - they are now pointing guns at us..."

Lisha muttered something as she once again stepped up the speed with the car following them - matching their speed - soon - the brown car was running parallel to them as it sped through the wrong lane & the car came dangerously close...

"Think of something Chaits - and quick..." Lisha screamed, "these belong to the group that attacked us yesterday..."

"How do you know?"

"They want your bag - that's what the guy's screaming about."

Chaits desperately racked his brain trying to see how he could get rid of these guys - he opened the top of the glass & pulled out a marble "Lisha - if I say stop - pull the emergency brake - if not keep driving at this speed..."

"Ok - what are you going to do?" said Lisha not looking at him - at this speed she needed to concentrate on the road. Chaits waived them to come closer & shouted "The brakes failed - we can't stop!"

They were unable to hear what he said & came closer - Chaits knew he had only one chance to pull it off & allowed them to come closer up to almost at an arm's length - he moved swiftly & threw the marble at the driver's face - the impact was huge as the marble hit the driver on his face & he lost control & veered off... The car somersaulted few times before coming to rest - upside down.

"That was great thinking, Chaits - but not enough - we have another car chasing us..."

"I hope they didn't notice what happened to the other car to topple like this..."

The other car came by their side & Chaits hurled another marble at the driver - "Lisha! Stop."

Lisha put on her emergency brakes even as the car lurched their way - first bumping its rear onto the front of their car & toppling over into the divider ditch sideways...

"I hope no more cars are following us - just one more marble left."

"No more" said Lisha laughing as they picked up speed again - Lisha veered off the expressway again & hit a small road... "They know what road we've taken & they're waiting for us almost everywhere on the expressway - this is a small detour - we'll circle around & enter KAL from the other side..." she said as she pulled in at a gas station for a wash & to check the damage to her car. They sat in a small restaurant keeping a wary eye for any suspicious car following them - sure that they were not being followed, they started off again & cruised on the smaller roads till they hit a road which was bumpy & passed through the dense forest...

"Wow! This jungle is very dense" Chaits looked around at the greenery, "any wild animals?"

"Not many here - few monkeys, few Snakes & lots of birds..."

## CHAPTER SIXTEEN

They cruised along through the jungle & travelled quite a bit without any incidence - they came to a T junction where a raw mud road entered the deeper jungle - Lisha took a turn into the deeper jungle - Chaits could see nothing except dense forest - suddenly - they came to a clearing & lo! - Chaits saw a beautiful log house, big enough to accommodate a group of ten people as guests...

"Wow!" he exclaimed.

"I told you my father works for the forest department - the government built such beautiful houses for guests with all amnesties in different parts of forests in this country. Currently - he's in another forest working on habitat there - he's gone for about six months & this house will be empty till he returns..."

"Wow! You're lucky to have a father who's got access to such good houses - you must be proud of him."

"I am" she said holding her head high - she fished out a key, opened the lock & smiled stepping in, "Welcome..."

Chaits looked at modern interiors and amenities "Hey how do you get water & electricity here?"

"You saw the forest going uphill - that's on the back of the house, that's the mountain which you've already visited... Yes - it's Genting - you remember the casino? - the supply of electricity & water comes from there - rather - the electricity is tapped out of the wire mesh from which electricity is supplied to the casino..."

"Um - hmm" Chaits desperately tried to understand this long sentence.

"We normally store canned food here - enough to last 3 months for a family as well we have solar energy & heaters installed for emergency!

"Lovely setup" "Chaits concluded.

He looked around as she showed the place to him - it was grand - 5 guest bedrooms - 2 host bedrooms - a large hall with a dining table for more than 10 people - exotic kitchen - lush bathrooms - a visible clearing of about 15ft on each side - loaded with amnesties like satellite TV & Internet - more like a plush 5 star accommodation - one look outside any window showed breath taking serene forest beauty - Chaits kept on clicking photos on his mobile trying to capture the serene beauty...

"Have you finished clicking your photos?" she asked a bit impatiently," I need some help. The cans of food are stored in the loft & I'm unable to reach it."

Chaits returned giving a sheepish smile, "Here - let me do that for you" he looked at a small stool that was about 1ft height & climbed on it - he wasn't able to reach the loft either - he looked around for something better - he climbed down & approached her - without warning her - he bent down & lifter her & climbed on the stool...

"Hey! What're you doing?" she asked laughing playfully.

"Are you able to reach the loft now?"

"I can now peep into it - thanks." she collected the cans she wanted, "now please put me down. There's something I like about you... You always come up with one solution or other - however - weird the solution is..." Chaits laughed at that sentence & sat on a chair watching her cook dinner for them - his mind automatically started sizing her up - it was his old habit that refused to die - he imagined a happy married life with her, how she'll cook food for him - how they'll enjoy the rest of their life - etc...

"Dinner's ready - you dreamy eyes" she said snapping him out of his day dreams - she was a good cook & they ate with huge appetite.

"Do we go to KAL tomorrow?" he asked - his heart sinking - if they reach KAL - he'd have to return to India & may not be able to meet her again - ever...

"No - we'll put up here for a couple of days - they must be watching all roads leading into KAL - If we don't show up for a couple of days - they'd think we plan to cross the border by road somewhere else & would relax their vigil."

Chaits was happy at heart - it wasn't a time to say good bye - yet... Chaits prodded her to speak more about self - and she gladly obliged by relating her past - right from her childhood amid a good wine she served... Chaits kept on listening to her without any interruption - he was getting to know her better as an individual.

"Which room do I occupy?" he asked in a sleepy tone - he looked at the watch - It was almost 2AM - she pointed to a door... "Thanks - good night & sweet dreams" he wished her sleepily & entered the room - he looked at the soft double bed & wished Lisha would share it with him - he managed to change into shorts & was deep asleep within moments...

He opened his eyes to the chirping of birds & blinked at the bright sunlight that filled the room - he looked at the clock on the wall 10.30AM - he'd slept soundly & felt a bit ashamed to wake up so late... His could smell a feminine perfume & a shampoo - he felt a soft hand pull him back into the bed & looked to his side - to his amazement & glee - he found Lisha sleeping soundly - next to him - her soft long hair partially hid her face as the tresses spread around & almost tickled his neck - she wore a soft baby pink nightie that looked messed up in her sleep showing her curves off to an advantage - he glanced downward - the bed covers hid her body but a bare leg protruded out showing him how shapely her legs were - her arm was outstretched as she softly put it around him in an embrace - he ogled at her beauty shamelessly for some more time - but controlled his instincts to put an arm around her & kiss her...

'No' he said to himself, 'I'm not a person who'd take undue advantage of the situation - she's here - because she trusts me & I'm alive - because I trust her...' With heavy heart, he gently lifted her arm & got out of the bed - he entered the bathroom with his toothbrush & looked at himself – 'Hey what's this?' he could identify the marks of her lipstick on his chest... 'Maybe, the wine got better of her...' he thought - though thrilled at this find, 'I need to observe her more - don't want to lose a friend like her and he carried on with his morning chores.

He stepped out of the bathroom - fresh. He found her - still soundly asleep - looking all the more attractive as the bed covers heaved with every breath she inhaled - he moved over to the window & pulled the curtains over to mellow the bright sunlight that may disturb her sleep... He entered the kitchen & prepared tea, put butter on the slices of bread she'd brought with them - put them in a tray & carried it to the bedroom - she opened an eye at him as he entered...

"Good Morning" he said smiling & presented the tray to her, "Surprize – bed tea for you"

"Oh! So sweet of you" she smiled at him & he watched her sip the tea & slip into the bathroom...

"What's our plan for the day?" he asked her as she cooked food for them.

"Well - actually - nothing - we're not going anywhere - unless you want to explore the jungle."

"Great idea... but, what about the snakes?"

"Leave them to me - we'll go when you're ready."

He put on his shoes as soon as they finished lunch, "I'm ready" he looked as Lisha wound a thick roll of cloth around his shin.

"This will keep the snake bites away if not the snakes" Chaits gulped at the thought - she wound a similar cloth on her legs underneath a designer gown that she miraculously produced from a bedroom in the house it was a fabulous top in baby pink with printed red flowers on it - she tied a nylon rope all around her waist & tied a butterfly knot on her left - this helped her show off her exclusive curves - the top fell over laced swishy skirt which ballooned - making it easy to walk & dropped down to her shin - below which was covered by the cloth she wound to fend away snake bites topped with sport shoes - she looked-straight out of a movie...

"Wow! Lisha - you look great."

"Don't be silly "she brushed him off as she blushed at his compliment - she held his hand as they walked in the forest & Chaits as usual captured the serene beauty of the forest along with her as the centre subject of his photographs.

"What's the rope on your waist for?"

"You can't predict rain around here - especially - this season - so in case it rains hard & quick sand is formed - this will pull us out of it..."

Fortunately - it didn't rain & they happily roamed around, 'Adam & Eve - with clothes' Chaits daydreamed & kept on smiling - by sundown - they returned - the fresh air of the jungle had revived their energy.

"Lisha" Chaits turned on his charm as he spoke to her, "you told me a lot about yourself - your school - your college - about 2 years of compulsory military training - but, when I look at you - I always get carried away by your beauty - you're so attractive - I'm sure boys would've been doing every trick in the trade to win your love - you skipped that part..."

She looked at him & his heart sank as her eyes turned dreamy for a moment "Yo - you're right - I was always hounded by boys & it thrilled me at first - but then it was troublesome - except for the girl's room - I was followed everywhere - there were few who even dared to publicly touch me - the dirty way - that's when my dad decided that I should learn Kung Fu - in about a year's time - I was famous as a bully girl - they called me 'oriental tigress" she laughed as she remembered her past.

"You mean to say - you never fell in love?"

"Um - no" she said after a thoughtful pause, "now that I think of it - it was not love... You can call it a silly crush or maybe - infatuation - never been in love during that time - I was not that girly - girly kind - I was more into finishing my graduation, learning Kung Fu was a passion & practising Kung Fu on those stupid boys was a delight..."

"What about after that?"

"As I finished my college - the goal of my life was clear - I didn't want to become somcone's wife & grow his children - I wanted to be my own self - so I concentrated learning tourism & travelled almost every country in east Asia - learnt local languages - I know most of them - perfect - and now I realise - I love to travel" she looked at Chaits, "why are you smiling?"

"Oh! I love to smile."

"Don't give me that crap - now I know you enough - to know what your smiles mean - out with it..."

"Ok - you win - I still am not ready to believe that you never fell in love or got attracted to a man - the whole of your life - look at me - I've more girlfriends than I can count - I still get easily attracted to beautiful dames - married or single - all the same - I find you a lively a person as I am..."

Her eyes dreamy again, she sighed... "Well - you never give up - do you? Recently I met someone that made my heart go weak - I know - it was an Infatuation at First Sight..." Chaits was all ears now & his undaunted attention flattered her as she continued. "I have a very cool head & that never gets blinded by my heart - this not the first time that I was infatuated by someone - so - I first started talking to him - then by chance - I had a chance to spend some time with him - I found that he's very good person by heart - but is utterly flirtatious - just like you..."

"Me?" he asked incredulous.

"Ya - just like you - if given a chance- he'll jump in bed with every girl he meets - he's strong, he's smart & handsome."

"Just like me." Chaits interrupted.

"Umm - ok - I'll give that credit to you" she said laughing, "and for heaven's sake take that silly charm out - I read it clearly - won't work with me..."

Chaits sat still, made some gargling sound of his throat, "Ok - the charm has been turned off."

"There - you're more attractive & charming - when you are yourself."

"What about this charming guy you met?"

"Sometimes - I hate your persistence" she said looking a bit angry - though she wanted Chaits to carry on...

"I'm just interested to know - now that you're told me so much - I won't be able to sleep..."

She laughed, "Ok - actually I've never been comfortable confiding my innermost feelings - but I think I'll try..."

"It's wrong to bottle up feelings, someday - you may regret that you never tried, go on- I promise you solemn secrecy" he could see that she wanted to get her feelings out - her dreamy eyes showed - he could see her struggling to get it out "Ok - take your time - I'll not insist further - I know you've never been able to bring out your feelings - but the day you do that I promise you - you'll be the happiest person on this earth..."

"Thank you, Chaits" she wiped off a tear that over flowed, "all these years of hard Kung Fu training & 2 years of rigorous army training has made me control all my emotions - it's really hard for me."

He put a comforting arm around her & pecked her on her cheek, "You still are very beautiful" she hugged him & started to weep & Chaits let her weep then she vanished into her bedroom leaving Chaits... wondering if he'd done the right thing - he put on the TV - sound muted and watched a movie which played in some local language - soon - he was totally engrossed in the action...

"You hungry?" Lisha asked as she stepped out of her bedroom - she looked as if she'd been crying all the time & had just washed her face to hide those tears...

Chaits got up & hugged her to comfort her, "Hey! I'm sorry - I didn't mean to make you cry like this..." he said softly.

"Shut up - Chaits" she said, looked at him, smiled & hugged him tight, "Thank you - now I know that I'm a human like you & not a machine."

"Knowing this - yes - I'm hungry."

After the dinner, he realised that he still was in the gear for his forest trek - he changed into his regular sleeping shorts & a sleeveless T-shirt - as he entered the main hall - he saw that Lisha had changed into her nightdress as well... His heartbeats accelerated when he saw her eyes widen & the look 'Impressed by Him' in her eyes - she was on the computer - checking her emails - he couldn't understand as it was in some oriental script.

"Hey! I haven't checked my emails for long..." he suddenly realized that his brother may have tried to contact him via email.

"Would you like to sip a hot tea?"

"Oh! That'd be lovely..."

"Ok - the computer is all yours." she said & walked into the kitchen.

He checked for any email from his brother - there was none - many from his friends...

"That's a different email id than you have on your card" she said as she sat next to him.

"This is my personal email - it's linked to my Facebook & other social sites & community sites as well - what you got was my office email ID on my visiting card."

"Oh! - is it ok - if I keep in touch with you on this email?"

"Definitely - I was going to tell you to exactly do that..."

"Chaits?" she sounded a bit inquisitive...

"What?"

"This girl, the good luck charm girl - you met at the casino - she must be rich - I've a doubt on her story about collecting money to repay her father's loan & buy freedom."

"Why do you say that?"

"The pendant she gifted you is made of costly gold."

Chaits was glad - this was the first time she had thought & behaved like a girl - she had noticed the pendant gifted by Laila - he could also sense some jealousy seeping in her tone...

"She wore this pendant when I met her - it belongs to her mother - she showed me her family photo - her mother wore this pendant."

"Would you mind if I take a closer look?" she said as she touched it...

"No problems - nothing to hide" he said as he removed it & handed it over to her - she curiously inspected it - "Chaits!" she screamed...

"What?" Chaits asked as he signed out of his email account.

"These are two pendants - not one."

"What do you mean?"

"Do you see this jade with a small ring around it? That's pendant number one & the big fat gold heart - it's been pasted to the jade & it's hollow."

"So what about it?" he asked as she shook the pendant.

"There's something inside it - wait for a moment I'll get tweezers - if she's working for those crooks who've been trying to kill you - this may contain a miniature transmitter and that's why they were able to find as - no matter where..."

Chaits sat straight - holding it as if he was holding a bomb - his heart not ready to believe that Laila could be associated with those terrorists - yet, he couldn't deny the possibility...

## CHAPTER SEVENTEEN

'How could such a sweet girl like Laila be associated with terrorists?' his heart was refusing to believe any possibility - he sat still & held the pendant waiting for Lisha to return.

"I got the tweezers & some other tools - let me have a look at that..." Lisha said as she snatched the pendant from him "Chaits, is she beautiful?" Chaits was accustomed to the concern in this voice when a girl asked it - he browsed through the photos in his mobile & showed her the photo which he had clicked at the casino - she looked at it for a long moment - shook her head as she let out a sigh of gloom...

"I know these kind of girls - they always want to latch on to good guys - they've no character..." she had a scorn of jealousy in her tone - Chaits knew this well - he didn't speak a word & looked at Lisha who avoided his glance & deliberately concentrated on the pendant - Chaits smiled knowingly & she frowned knowing that Chaits was able to understand her innermost feelings - easily...

"Ah-ha" she exclaimed as the jade was prized out of the thick hollow gold pendant - sure enough - they were two different pendants & Chaits held his breath as Lisha worked upon dissecting the large gold pendant - after a short struggle - she managed to unlock & open it - inside - both the walls were occupied by faces of & cute girls - Chaits did recognize that photo - it was Laila & her sister - a small packet wrapped in paper fell out... Chaits bent, picked it up & he carefully opened the tiny packet.

"Hey - this looks like a mini sized memory card of a mobile phone."

"Ya - sure looks like it - I wonder what it contains..."

"Wait - I got a card reader" he said getting up & returned with his multi-card reader.

"Chaits... The paper you unwrapped - it seems like a small letter - what's that about?"

"Let's read it." Lisha shifted her position so as to sit behind him & read it along with him.

'Dear Chaits' the letter read 'Since I grew up - I've met men - a lots of them - all of them were lusty for having sex with me & had no consideration for me as a human being - You - are the first I met who is different & respects women.'

"See - I'm not as bad as you think."

"That's the reason - we're here together - so - stop blowing your trumpet & read on..."

"How do you know that?"

"Ever heard of a woman's instinct?" she repeated her question the way she had when they had walked along on the Penang beach for the first time - Chaits wondered for a moment as to what did she mean but carried on reading Laila's letter...

'I was approached by a lusty, mean looking man who offered me 5K MYR to keep you occupied for the night - his name is Jamil - I've seen him around with many other mean looking men - they don't seem like normal casino visitors - they look more like gangsters. At first, I thought you would turn out to be the normal lusty fellow who I need to seduce & take to my room - so I told Han to mix your drink & drug you off to sleep - I think our other boss, Mr Wong, has some sinister links with them - when he pointed you out to me -

I felt bad because I'd seen you enter the casino & I'd liked you...'

Lisha muttered something in local language which Chaits didn't understand - but knew instantly that she was swearing at Laila... he read on... 'It was when I actually approached you - I understood that you were a very good person by heart & when you asked me to Trust GOD & have faith in Him - I was in two minds...'

"Liar" Lisha muttered.

'I wanted to tell you the reason why I approached you - I'd overheard them - they were planning to search your room while I kept you occupied - on second thought - I didn't want you to go back to your room - because they'd have killed you. So I took you to my room - I really want to thank you for giving me the confidence to get out of this rotten job & these rotten men - they were expecting you to return around noon - but you returned in about a couple of hours & they had to run for it...'

"Hmm - I didn't know you're so good at heart - someday - you can be a Priest" Lisha's joy was imminent as she put her arm around him.

'I couldn't sleep after you left & felt worried about you - so I snooped around their room - I overheard them... they spoke about some USB that they searched in your room.'

"What's all about this USB that I haven't even seen?" Chaits feigned his musing & read on...

'They were very angry on me because I wasn't able to keep you occupied for long - they were planning to kidnap you - torture you till they get the USB & then kill you. Chaits - I've been a false Lucky Charm Girl for everyone - but I pray - I really want to be a Real Lucky Charm for you - so that you can return to India - safe.'

"Oh! How touching?" Lisha said in concerned voice.

'Chaits - I don't know - if I'll be alive when you read this - but I'll die a happy girl - trying not to give out any information about you - please - GO BACK TO YOUR HOME & YOUR FAMILY - I managed to take photographs of most people associated with them - please check the memory card that I put along with this letter... knowing them may save your life - I do wish I had met you before I joined this casino - Han will email you the news of my death - so long – Chao...'

"God" said Lisha, "I wish, I'd noticed this pendant when I picked you up at Penang - I'd have brought you to KAL even before they realized..." she hugged him tighter in concern, "Did you receive any email from Han?"

"I've not spoken to her much - she wouldn't know my email id - unless..."

"Unless, what?" she screamed.

"Oh! My God! Lisha - I'd given my business card to Laila - if they get hold of it - they'd be able to trace me - all the way to Mumbai."

"You & your instincts to impress girts" Lisha sounded desperate, "I hope she destroyed your card before they got her - on second thought - she may have handed it over to Han - have checked your business email id?"

"No - I haven't" Chaits turned back to the computer & logged into his business account - he furiously searched for Han's email... Sure enough there was an unread email from her - he opened it...

'Hi Chaits - I'm sorry I won't be able to write in detail - after you left those bastards have locked her in her room & are torturing her to know more about you - she's going to be shipped out next Sunday to Bankok where she'll be branded as a prostitute - the thing she hates the most - this is going to be her punishment for helping you - poor girl suffers torture for your sake - I do hope you reach safely to India - I'm destroying your card even as I type this - please pray for her soul...'

"BASTARDS" they both screamed in unison.

"Lisha - my life means nothing - anyways - the chances of them finding & killing me are high - and if I have to die - I'd like to have a noble death - trying to save a poor girl from clutches of those bastards..."

"Chaits don't be sentimental - this email was sent on the same day you left Genting - she may by now be at Bangkok or even worse - dead - please do not let her sacrifice go waste."

"I'll find out" Chaits said determined, "no one gives or puts life in danger for me & not find me helping her - I'll call Han & find out."

"That'll only alert them - I'll call Han on your behalf & find the information for you do you have their phone number?"

"Sure - I do - I liked the place so much that I wanted to visit again - with you..." he got up & got their card & tariff leaflet - Lisha looked at the name on email "she seems to be a Korean."

She dialled the number & spoke in Korean language that's what Chaits thought - he couldn't make out one oriental language from other - after a pause she spoke again - she put the phone down & smiled.

"She's still a captive at Genting they're going to take her to Bangkok in next 2-3 days"

"I'm going back there & try to rescue her. Can you lend me a torch?" Chaits said decidedly.

"Why?"

"You said the hill behind this house leads there I'll go there tonight..."

"Don't be short sighted Chaits - we'll go there tomorrow night & rescue her."

"No - Lisha - I'm not allowing you there."

"You can't stop me. If you go alone - I'll follow you – so - it's better that we work out a plan with a cool head - we have a better chance of succeeding - that way..."

Chaits thought & found her way more reasonable, "Let's first look at the faces of our enemy so that we can identify them in the crowd."

He put the memory card in the reader & looked at a folder 'Bad Guys' he opened it & they memorised the faces as they appeared... Lisha recognised one of them who now lay in the valley near Kek Lok Si temple - Chaits recognised another - he was in the first car that toppled over on the expressway.

"Who are these girls in yellow?"

"They're the Lucky Charm Girls - I really don't know how many - but I do know that there are too many of them."

"I have an idea Chaits - If I can get hold of that dress - I can roam around inside the premise - whoever sees me will think that I'm one of them that way we can find Laila."

"Good idea - that way - you'll be safe."

"The problem is - how do I get that uniform? - who'll give it to me?"

"I can get it for you... I know a shop in KAL that sells these dresses - if we can go there - we can buy it."

"Great - so we go to KAL in the morning - buy the dress & then proceed to Genting Highlands."

"I suggest we go there late in the evening - the best time for us will be about 3 to 4AM - by then most of their men will be sleepy & the guard will be lower..."

They slept after they revised their plan - again & again...

## CHAPTER EIGHTEEN

Chaits counted the money, he still had with him 67000 MYR - he kept 47k back & carried 20K - he had to show that he had lots of money to spend at casino - he planned to keep 15k for Laila & loose the rest if the day was bad... He wore his batik shirt underneath a jacket & comfortable jeans ready for action - he took his bag which held his roller skates.

"You won't need that" Lisha told him as she opened the door on her way out - he kept the bag on the sofa & followed her out... "They'll know our car by now - so we're going on a bike" she said & opened the door to a second garage - Chaits looked at a beautiful bike which proclaimed its power & speed - just by its look...

"Wow! Is that yours?"

"No - belongs to my father - but I normally use it when I'm around"

"I would like to ride this one"

"No – Chaits - you don't possess a local driving licence"

"Please, Lisha - inside the forest till we reach the main road"

"Ok - but be careful"

Chaits rode the bike till main road & got a wonderful feel of its power. It really was a powerful machine - as they approached the main road - they switched positions - they were glad - the helmets they wore would hide their faces from the terrorists who were on the lookout. They wouldn't recognise them...

"Are you sure you'll be able to ride this?" Chaits asked a bit concerned.

"Don't worry, she said buckling her jacket - just hold tight" & she accelerated the bike with a huge wheelie & they sped toward KAL.

'She's a daredevil of rider' Chaits thought as he held her tight - soon he was comfortable as his confidence on her riding skills grew - he released his firm hold around her waist... Once in KAL - they didn't waste any time - she dropped him at a saloon on the way, entering through the back door & instructed her friend to disguise his look while she sped off to buy the Lucky Charm Girl dress...

She returned in an hour's time "Where's Chaits?" she asked looking around.

"I'm right in front of you" Chaits said.

"Oh! My God! This is brilliant nobody will recognise you. You look perfectly originated in East Asia - remember - you're mute & cannot speak"

She disappeared in changing room & re-appeared wearing the Lucky Charm Girl dress. Chaits couldn't help ogling at her - she looked absolutely stunning & sexy in that dress...

"Thank you Chaits - you look full of lust told me how I look..." she said & laughed - she changed into her riding gear again & packed her dress in a paper bag - now they were on their way to rescue Laila - his heart beating silently...

As they reached Genting Highlands, Chaits guided her toward parking lot for bikes. He pointed to the spot nearest to the main door which housed the rooms of the Lucky Charm Girls... Chaits explained the layout of that building to her & she nodded...

"That's Han over there at the bar - she'll help you change your dress & see if she knows where Laila is…"

Chaits murmured a prayer & hoped that everything will go well - he put on a silly smile on his face as he entered the casino - he waited for the main guy who allocated the Lucky Charm Girls to enter the tokens room for something & deliberately counted the money - slowly - making the guy think that he'd lots to loose. He counted 5000 & put the rest back in the small shoulder sack he carried - he looked around & slowly went around to the poker counter & bought the coupons - satisfied at the guy's attention - on his way out he looked at the bar - Abdul was not there. He went over to the poker table & waited for his turn in the meantime, he deliberately ogled at all the girls to check if Laila was around by any chance - he wished that she was there. It would be easy to get her out this way - rather than searching for her - she was not to be seen…

He resigned himself to playing poker - last time he wasn't bothered - this time - he wanted desperately to win - win huge amount. He played on & soon started winning - he was happy - he'd won about 50K when the table broke - he cashed it keeping the 5k coupons with him - he went out of peeped in the restaurant to signal Lisha…

Lisha was ready & all dressed up like a Lucky Charm Girl. She followed him discreetly into the casino she looked at the main guy & approached him - "Hi! I'm a new joiner - I'm supposed to demonstrate my charms tonight - so please guide me…"

The guy's eyes almost fell off looking at her as he nervously licked his lips trying to control his lust for her - he looked around & saw the person operating the poker table point at Chaits - then signed that Chaits had won over 100K…

"Look at that sucker on the poker table - he's winning high hands - make him play more so that he loses & let me know when you feel that he wants to leave" she nodded & approached Chaits.

"You need to walk more seductively" a senior girl advised, "watch me as I approach my sucker" & she walked away with seductive sway of hips - Lisha looked at her & imitated - the guy smiled his approval - his eyes still lusty for her. Lisha approached the table & put a soft hand on Chaits' shoulder - Chaits looked at her - she smiled at him & spoke in local language - repeating in English.

"Hey! Handsome, would you like to use me as your Lucky Charm? - I've been lucky for many guys like you - but - I like you the most..." She spoke this in such a sexy tone, that Chaits was taken aback for a moment - he looked at her head to toe in approval of her act & nodded his consent - she smiled at him, put on arm around his shoulder & sat on his lap - she looked at the main guy who showed Thumbs Up. Chaits played on & won another 50K - he looked at his watch - 3AM - he tapped Lisha on her thigh - she got up & briskly walked back to the main guy...

"Fantastic!" he approved, "what's that sucker saying?"

"He's mute - he can't speak - but I think he wants to quit & go back"

"Check if he's booked in for stay - if not show me thumbs down - quick..."

Lisha approached Chaits again & spoke again in the local language & English - Chaits shook his head in denial - she made a baby face & hugged him showing the main guy a thumbs down - he beckoned her to come back at the counter...

"Good girl - you're earned your commission for today. I'll give you a bumper incentive of 500 MYR - if you make him stay & play tomorrow..."

"What do I have to do?" she asked making her eyes wide at the mention of 500 MYR.

"He seems to like you. Take him to bed with you & make him enjoy sex with you. You can charge up to 500 MYR which is yours to keep."

"Oh!" she feigned horror & put her hands behind her & crossed her fingers - it was a sign for Chaits. They'd now be able to enter the building where he'd last met Laila - he was at the last hand of that table and waited for others to raise the stake...

"Now - baby - don't worry - with your looks & attitude - I promise you will make it big - you'll soon get used to this & will start enjoying as you collect money" he laughed....

"Ok" she said a bit toned down..." he hasn't booked a stay & I don't have a room - how will I do it?" she asked him innocently.

"Don't worry about that - we had a Star girl, her name was Laila - but she betrayed us - she's still in her room - I'll vacate that room & give her room to you. You can be our Star girl as her replacement & enjoy her benefits - go take that sucker before he leaves will all the money. The room is in the building next to parking lot for the bikes & the room no is 106 - all the best." he pushed her toward Chaits & patted her behind much to her annoyance. She ignored it approached Chaits again - sensuously swaying her hips as she walked toward him. She seemed excited.

"Good news - I found her - she's in room 106 - we're supposed to enjoy sex in the same room - they're going to take Laila out of there & put us in her place - Now's our chance to save her." she whispered excitedly & put her hand around him "Please - don't go, handsome - she turned on her sexy tone again, wouldn't you like to spend a night with me?"

Chaits ogled at her again & nodded.

"Wait here - I'll get the key to my room" she went back to the guy & reported.

"You take him to the room - I'll instruct that the room needs to be vacated for you"

"What about the girl in there?"

"Oh! Don't worry about her - we'll lock her in the store room – go – go – go..."

"I don't have the key"

"Don't worry there are 2 guys guarding that door - they'll open it for you - take him there in 30 minutes - see if he'd want a drink - we'll have enough time to vacate the room by then."

She returned to Chaits & held his hand and pulled him out of casino "We need to hurry - got 30 minutes before they vacate the room."

They started walking along the corridors, "Chaits you have good acting skills - you did pretty well since we entered what happened to you now?"

"Nothing, why?"

"You had that typical smile off mischief when I told you that we're succeeded in plan & you still have the smile ... you're not acting that good..."

"Um – pardon me for that - for a moment I thought" he said in a low voice as Lisha took his arm & put it around her waist...

"Hey - what're you doing?"

"Remember - I still am the Lucky Charm girl here & you're a lusty sucker and yes - what did you think?"

"Well" he paused dramatically - he was still keeping his voice low remembering he was supposed to be a mute, "I thought..." and stopped as they passed a worker in the corridor. "I thought you were excited at the thought of enjoying sex with me – ouch - that hurt..."

Lisha poked a strong elbow in his ribs, "I'll let you know my reaction to this once we return to my forest home - now hold me as if you're lusty - else, you may ruin the whole plan."

"You know I'm not like that..."

"Oh! Ya? I remember how you put your hand around my waist when we rode the bike."

"Oh - that was a friendly touch."

"Shut up - Chaits - and play your part well - we have to get Laila out of here" she said as they came out of the main building to cross over... They both looked at their bike - it was parked quite near to the entrance & there was nothing that would be a hurdle when they made a run for it - they paused outside the main door of the building as they quickly put on their act together - Chaits started fondling her as they walked to the elevator...

"Here keep the key of bike in your pocket - all the best to us" she said her face grim. They put on the act again as they alighted & Chaits pointed toward the room - sure - it was the same room at the end of the corridor - they both wondered - if they had to run - they'll have to cross the entire corridor - and it wasn't going to be easy... There were two people guarding the room & they looked at the couple coming toward them with disinterest - it was something they were accustomed to...

"Hi" Lisha said with a smile & handed over a small chit - they read it & got up - one of them started searching his pocket for the key while the other looked at Lisha with lusty eyes - Lisha smiled at him & poked Chaits on his ribs as the other guy turned around & inserted the key to the door - Chaits waited for him to press the unlock code & the door to open. As soon as the door opened he tapped at the unsuspecting man - he turned around in time to receive one of the finest knockout punches in the boxing history – he fell down - unable to make any sound.

The other guy was taken by surprise - Lisha hit out a firm kick between his legs & then a vicious chop behind his neck knocking him off. Chaits held them with their collars & pushed the room open & dragged in two unconscious men in… there, they tied and gagged them.

"I told you I know nothing about him - please stop torturing me – let me go" a voice shrieked in horror as they entered - Chaits turned around even as Lisha shut the door - they looked at the girl who was shrieking in horror - Chaits couldn't believe his eyes while Lisha felt pity for Laila - her hair seemed messed up, obviously they seemed to be pulled at mercilessly - her face looked swollen from the slaps she'd received & from the tears she had cried - her arms were black & blue - she must have been hit several times with a stick or something similar.

"Shut her up - while I change clothes" Chaits sat next to Laila & kept a firm hand on her mouth to stop her from shrieking again…

"Shh-shh" he comforted her, 'now-now - calm down - we're here to help you" he said in a soothing voice & she stopped screaming & shaking - her eyes had seen hope for a fraction of a second - but the horror of torture was still playing on her mind -

"I know that voice" she said trying to remember, "who - who are you – and - why do you want to help me?" she was still uncertain of the couple who'd entered her room…

"We are here to help you" Lisha said softly sitting on the other side next to her while Chaits washed off his makeup - he was feeling uncomfortable about it…

"You're one of them - I saw your Lucky Charm Girl uniform - how can I believe you?"

"At least you can believe me" Chaits said as he wiped of his wet face with a towel.

She looked at him for a moment as he crossed over and sat next to her - then she remembered "Chaits - is that really you?" Chaits nodded, "oh - I asked you to get out of this country - why did you return? - I risked my life to save yours..."

"And did you believe that I'll run away like a coward when I know that you're in danger - simply because you tried to save my life?" he smiled.

Her eyes showed tremendous relief as she hugged him "Oh! Chaits - you shouldn't have returned - many girls like me need to meet a good guy like you & take inspiration to lead a good, normal life - the world is full of unlucky girls like me they need your help..."

"Now that I'm here - let me first help you out of this situation - after that I'll worry about other girls like you - c'mon - we're getting out of here..."

Lisha got up & opened her wardrobe - selected a simple top & a trouser which will attract less attention... They stood still as they heard a soft knock on the door - Chaits dashed at Laila & put a firm hand over her mouth to stop her from screaming & nodded at Lisha...

"Who is it?" she asked in irate tone "Oh! Fine - it's you - the new girl - are you ok with the sucker? Where's he?"

"He's in the bathroom"

"Good - and where's the other girl?"

"I don't know - 2 people out there dragged her off - she was screaming something..."

"They must have taken her to the store - good luck - I want the guy to play again & lose."

There was an awkward silence - Lisha tiptoed to the door & silently opened it & peeped out "He's gone" she whispered "where's the store?"

"It's in the main building a bit far off - will take about 35 minutes of walk" Laila informed

"Here" Lisha threw the clothes she'd picked from the wardrobe, "Get into these quickly - we don't have much time..."

Laila didn't bother getting into bathroom to change - she didn't have enough strength & her body ached - Lisha held Chaits' hand in concern - Laila had removed her top & her entire body seemed to be marked with scars of the torture she'd endured - the sight was really heartrending - she managed to painfully change her clothes. She tried to get up but the pain was too much for her...

"Chaits - I think you need to carry her. I'll guard your path - lift her up - what're you waiting for, Christmas?"

Chaits lifted Laila in his arms as Lisha cautiously opened the door & peeped out - she signalled him to follow they entered the elevator & once again Lisha signalled a free passage & they reached the main door which Chaits pushed open with his leg...

"STOP! Who goes there?" a voice shouted at them from behind - Chaits turned around with Lisha facing about 6-7 men with their guard batons...

"I'll handle them - take her out & start the bike - wait outside the door - I'll join you in a couple of minutes"

Chaits stepped out with Laila even as Lisha lashed out a fierce kick at the first guy - he almost ran carrying Laila to the bike - seated her & leapt on it in front of her - he started the bike even as he put the helmet on - he rushed toward the main door in time to see Lisha run out & avoid a baton that was thrown her way - she leapt on the bike behind Laila as Chaits accelerated & got the bike out of the campus even before the alarm was raised…

Now they were racing downhill on the curvy track - Chaits stretched out his arm with a spare helmet – "Lisha wear this - we're being followed…"

Lisha wore the helmet & grasped Chaits tightly & Laila sat sandwiched between, unable to move - Chaits raced on the curvy road & glanced at the rear - view mirror. There were 2 bikes chasing them - one of them quickly rode on so as they were now driving parallel to each other…

"Hold on" Chaits shouted pulling the tough plastic visor down to cover his face in time to avoid a blow on his face as the pillion on the bike other bike lashed a baton at him. He rode on a bit shaken by this sudden lash & cursed under his breath – 'I wish I had the marble in Lisha's car' he thought… Lisha looked at what was happening - Chaits was driving dangerous as he tried to avoid the baton - she threw the baton she had taken from the guard at the face of the rider of the other bike - he was not prepared for that & turned sharp to avoid the blow - his motion & speed made the bike take a somersault as both the people riding it flew, as if they imitated Superman into the darkness - while their bike fell over the side wall tumbling down - Chaits deftly managed a haırpın bend ahead & the sound of the screech the tyres made as they skid almost 180° turn seemed deafening in the silence…

He raced the bike again - knowing the other one was on his tail - he managed to avoid hitting the first bike that tumbled down on the road front of him - he looked into the rear view mirror again - the bike chasing them also had managed to avoid the bike which was now blazing with fire - to his dismay - he saw about 3-4 cars which also seemed to be chasing them. They were 2 turns behind him. The blaze on the bike must have hit the gasoline - it blew up in smithereens & gave him time as the cars in chase stopped - he'd have about 3-4 minutes of lead time when those cars clear the burning debris...

His immediate concern was the bike which was close behind him - he veered - one side to other - not allowing them to speed up come parallel to him...

"Lisha" he shouted "Ever played computer games?"

"Yes - what about it - now?"

"Remember - Road Rash?"

"Yes" she said picking up the clue "let that bike be parallel & close enough..."

"Good" said Chaits & stopped going side to side allowing the bike to come close & parallel.

"Chaits - hold on..." Lisha shouted stood on her left leg taking a firm grip on the foothold & held Chaits by his shoulder - she delivered a fantastic kick on the driver's face even as the bike skidded & hit the side of the mountain...

"Fantastic" Chaits shouted in joy - they reached a road junction at the base "which way?" he asked slowing down.

"The extreme right" Lisha said - Chaits turned & sped off - racing, knowing that cars would come in hot pursuit. Fortunately, they were on the other side of the hill & the bike's light couldn't be seen - the road was still curvy but a smoother one. He drove at high speed for about 20kms when Lisha pointed a right turn to him. He made the turn & realised that the road led to her forest house - it had started raining heavily now... he put the bike off after going in for about 100 metres...

"What happened?" Lisha asked. Chaits put a finger as his lips to silence her even as they heard a car come at top speed – true, a car approached the turn they had taken & whizzed off without noticing them...

"They'd have noticed the light of our bike" he explained, "good the rain will wash off any trail we may have left." He started the bike and they were soon inside the warmth of her forest house - Laila looked bad in shape as she fainted...

"Poor girl - those bastards should be shot." Lisha couldn't hide her hate for those bad men – "Help me put her in one of the bedrooms" Chaits gently put Laila on the bed & came out into the main hall to be joined in couple of minutes by Lisha who held Laila's wet clothes...

## CHAPTER NINETEEN

Lisha put the clothes away & prepared a hot nourishing soup for them – she went into Laila's room and fed her.

"How's she?" Chaits asked her in concern.

"Badly bruised but otherwise - fine - the medical soup will nourish her well - she should be fine by evening...

Chaits looked at the watch - 5AM - he was feeling sleepy but decided to keep awake - one of them had to be on guard.

Lisha then prepared her medical oil that had magical effect on Chaits when he had skated down the hill behind Kek Lok Si temple...

"Chaits - could you please help me open this door? I have this pan full of boiled oil..."

Chaits gladly helped her & peeped in - he could see Laila sleeping naked as Lisha had taken off her wet clothes - she was well covered by a warm sheet and her shapely leg did protrude out...

"Need any help?"

"I don't want your dirty hands touch her body" Lisha scorned at the idea, "get out - will you?"

Chaits smiled and made his exit as Lisha proceeded to apply the oil to Laila. After she finished, she tapped the door with her knee hoping Chaits had not gone off to sleep - she smiled in relief as Chaits pushed the door open - she stepped out quickly to stop Chaits peeping inside - Chaits pulled the door shut & relaxed on the sofa.

Lisha freshened up & looked around for Chaits - she found him still relaxing on the sofa, "Aren't you sleepy?"

"I'm - but I'm planning to stay awake while you sleep & keep a watch - just in case - they find us & attack. You're had a tough night yourself - go to sleep - I'll sleep when you wake up."

Lisha thought for a while & nodded - she entered the bedroom where they had kept their sacks. Chaits followed... "Now what?" she asked.

"I came to get my shorts & T-shirt. I'm still wearing my wet clothes."

"Oh! Ok, and wake me up if you need anything - there's lot of soup left - you can have it if you feel hungry..."

"Good night" he said as she looked at the watch showing 7AM & confused with what he said - but she was sleepy & didn't bother - she sat on the bed & pulled the cover up - she groaned in pain as she hit the bed...

"Hey - you ok?" Chaits asked in concern...

"Ya" she said but Chaits wasn't convinced - he entered the bathroom & seemingly closed the door - he changed his wet clothes keeping his ears open - he heard her groan again - he was convinced that all wasn't well. He came out of the bathroom & looked at her - she had closed her eyes & was trying to control the pain... He sat next to her & gently touched her forehead and caressed her temple & her soft hair - she opened a beautiful eye at him...

"It is okay - I'll be fine when I wake up."

He held her hand - his eyes showed concern for her "Don't lie to me" he said softly "let me see what's hurting you..."

"No it's ok"

"Lisha - I dont have enough words to thank you. You've stood by me - in every danger - knowing well that this may cost you your life" a tear rolled down his cheek...

"Hey - C'mon - tough boys like you don't cry - they don't look good when they cry" she said & sat as she hugged him - Chaits slowly ran his fingers through her soft hair onto her back - he softly groped her back for trace of the pain - at one point - she let out huge gasp, trying to stop her voice from screaming out in pain - he gently removed her top, turned her around - he could see some black and blue strips - resulted from some baton hits she had taken...

He gently laid her on her stomach "Stay as you are... don't put on your top" He rushed out & heated the medical oil she had applied to Laila & held the hot pan using a towel & rushed back.

"You don't have to do this for me Chaits"

"Shut up & don't move" he said, "Ouch!" his fingers almost burned in the hot oil - then he remembered how she had applied the hot oil to him - he dipped the chopstick into the oil & removed it... the oil that stuck onto it started dripping onto her sore points as he carefully poured it - drop by drop. Then he started gently massaging her bare back... the feeling was so good to Lisha - that she slept off soundly within minutes - Chaits checked her body for any other injuries - satisfied - he got up and covered her with a soft sheet of cloth & closed the door behind him as he entered the main hall.

He sat on the sofa with nothing to do... the sleep got better of him & he dozed off. He looked up with a start as a soft hand touched his forehead. "Would you like some tea?" Lisha asked with a smile - he looked at the watch - 5PM...

"Wow! I must have fell asleep - how are you?" she sat next to him & hugged him tight.

"Don't care for me so much" she said, tears rolling down her cheeks, "I'm not used to it - I've been alone & have learned to take care of myself - the hard way - please don't make me weak."

"That doesn't answer my question" he said turning her around. He rolled the back of her dress high - amazingly - the blacks & the blues had disappeared - he let the top fall back "You really have a magic medicine."

She smiled at him & pecked his cheek in joy, "I'll get some tea for you."

"Chaits" a voice called.

"Laila! She must have woken up" he said, "Lisha please give her a dress."

Lisha entered the bedroom where Laila was & returned - Freshen up Chaits - you still look sleepy. Chaits freshened up & entered the hall to see both of them busy in the kitchen - they were speaking in some local language which he didn't understand - he let them carry on & sat on the sofa - he put on the TV for news - it was again some language he didn't understand so he surfed channels till he reached a music channel that played Indian music - something he had missed since he'd stepped in Malaysia.

"A special Treat for you, Chaits" Lisha said as she walked in with Laila - both holding trays with variety of dishes.

"For all the good work that you've done"

"Well, what do we have here?"

"Speciality, Thai & Malay dishes that we could cook in the same kitchen" said Laila - she looked quite normal now...

"Hmm - looks yummy" he said rubbing his hands eager to eat - he realized he was hungry.

"You should know what Laila knows about those bad men" Lisha said concerned as they relaxed after a wonderful meal.

"Chaits" Laila started on a serious note, "I think - rather - we both think that you should leave this country - right now." Chaits looked at Lisha who nodded, "The bad guys who held me captive, are basically out to kill you. They are not just bad guys, they are terrorists"

"Terrorists? Here in Malaysia?"

"Yes - they seem to have made some dangerous plan - from what I overheard - they are planning a spate of bomb blasts - the plan was supposed to be brought in by some person who had travelled from Pakistan - he was to come here - but it seems he misplaced the pouch carrying a USB of their master-plan!"

"Oh! I see – Chaits, maybe they think the USB is with you" Lisha said.

"Exactly" asserted Laila, "they think that you are a Secret Agent from India"

"Me? a secret agent?" Chaits looked around in disbelief, "My God! They must be watching a lot of James Bond movies" he started laughing.

"Chaits!" Lisha said sternly, "this is serious - don't take it so lightly"

"Ok - alright - so I'm supposed to be James Bond from India - but in that case I should've been killing them with a gun & I haven't even seen how a real gun looks like... except when they pointed the guns at us..."

"They have their people placed in different offices of the government - including some women & girls - they investigated you - that way & now know that you're not..." Laila continued

"Wait - but how do you know all this?"

"When you left with your group - they captured me & started torturing me to know more about you - I'm not used to such kind of brutality & I fell unconscious - when I came back to senses - I pretended to be unconscious & that way - I was able to hear what they said or discussed - then I started to pretend every time they started to torture - just to avoid it - and heard a lot..."

"Good girl" Lisha smiled & patted her.

"They found this out when you visited the Indian Embassy - they have 2 people working there - unfortunately I don't remember their names - one of them is a lady - they visited these terrorists."

"Oh My God! Traitors! If I get to know who they are..." Chaits left the balance hanging, "On various occasions, they searched your baggage - they had decided to let you go since you had not approached the police about the man who had travelled from Pakistan & who they have killed..."

"So why are they behind me now?"

"By the time they decided to let you go - you were intercepted by their men in Penang - only one of them survived that made them think that you really were a secret agent from India who killed their men - and now - you returned & escaped with me - right under their nose - that'll make them absolutely livid."

"That means - I've put Lisha in great danger as well - they must have seen her."

"No - don't worry about that - her makeup was too good for anyone to recognise her - I was not at all able to tell the difference after she cleaned her makeup - and you'll agree that I know about the makeup better than anyone else..." everyone agreed.

"This clearly calls for only one action plan" Chaits got up - his decision made, "Lisha, Laila - get ready - we're leaving."

"Where?"

"First to any nearest place where Laila gets transportation - back to her home - from there - Lisha goes back to Penang & I go to the Indian Embassy - it's easier to argue with 2 people than fight entire army of unknown terrorists."

"You cannot go back to KAL " Laila said, "they have hundreds of men watching every entry into KAL"

"We did go into the heart of KAL to buy her the Charm Girl dress & into the Genting - they didn't notice."

"Now - they would - now they know that we've a bike - it's simply dangerous. The only way I think you'll be safe is here - in this forest house" Lisha said.

"I agree - but how long can I stay like this - and once my visa gets over - the police will start hunting for me - and then I'll have to run from two groups - the terrorists & the police..."

"What I'd suggest is - we should lie low here for few days - we'll come out with some plan." Lisha suggested

"I think" Chaits said "Laila will have to go back to her family - they'd be concerned - I'm sure those bastards will manage to break into her bank account - they must have all the details & know that she'll have to come back to them for her money."

"They don't have the address of my family - I never gave it to them - so if I stick around they'll never know" said Laila

"In fact that's the very reason you should return to your family as early as possible - they'll be pressed for money & may try to contact you at Genting - then - it'll be very easy for them to get your address - and you'll never be able to escape from them."

"Oh! My God! This never occurred to me" Laila said with concern, "You're right - I must return to my family before anything happens."

"First - call them from my mobile & let them know that you're returning" Lisha said handing her mobile - Laila made a call to let them know...

"That's it" Chaits got up, "let's move..."

They sat in Lisha's car & she drove away from KAL to some distant town where Laila was able to board a bus to her home - Chaits handed her a pouch filled with 5OK MYR before she boarded "This will take care of your father's loan & leave enough for you to start something of your own."

She hugged Lisha to thank her & then pecked Chaits for all his help "I'll never forget that I met you, Chaits" were her fading words...

## CHAPTER TWENTY

"I hope - she reaches safely." Lisha said with concern. "What was the hurry to send her off this way - she could still be in danger."

"I don't think so - they are on lookout for me - not her - when will that bus reach her hometown?"

"Maybe, sometime by tomorrow noon"

"We'll call & check - mind if I smoke?"

"No - carry on - after we fill in the fuel"

It was almost midnight when they returned "You still didn't answer my question - why did you send her off in such a hurry?"

"Lisha - I hope you understand... I'm in grave danger - sure to be mercilessly tortured & killed if they catch me - she's not a girl like you who's trained to fight - running around with her means - suicide - all of us would be killed - I don't want her killed after we saved her."

"What about me?" Lisha challenged.

Chaits smiled at that question & looked at her, "I've about 150K MYR still with me and I've a different plan for you - I'll never ever allow any danger to even touch your hair - if they have to kill, they'll kill me first even before they approach you."

Lisha put her hand softly over his mouth "Let's not talk of death - we'll live & kill those bastards"

"You're right - let's be positive - Buddha has blessed us when we visited the temple & that's why we're alive & together" Chaits said his voice full of faith & confidence as he mechanically put on the TV... he surfed through few channels & stopped at a news channel. Lisha sat straight as the news of horrible accidents on Genting hill road splashed - they were the bikes who had chased them the night before & then they showed a car that had been abandoned with a dead man - it was the main guy at the casino who allocated & managed the Charm girls...

"Chaits" Lisha asked slowly "you're not planning to leave your 150K with me & leave me alone & run away for fear of putting me in danger - are you?"

"How did you know?" Chaits asked not believing that she had managed to read his mind.

"Ever heard about a woman's instinct?" she repeated her mysterious question... She just looked at sky & shrugged then turned furiously at him, "Mr Chaits - don't ever think of doing that - I swear, I'll go back into that casino - with a gun this time & kill as many bastards that I can before they shoot me down - at least I'll die knowing that I'll have reduced the number of people trying to kill you. So, we stick together - or I carry out Hara-Kiri by attacking that casino - the choice is yours."

Chaits looked at her & knew she wasn't bluffing "Ok - we stick together..."

"Good boy - now let's catch up on our sleep and always remember what I decided."

Chaits started laughing & she looked at him in disbelief "Now what?"

"I was teasing you but I do have a plan for you which, I'll let you know at an appropriate time."

"What is it?" she was still not ready to believe him.

"Now-now - don't look at me like that I promise I'll not run away from you & always stick by your side. You taught me what true friendship means. I'll be with you - always."

Chaits changed over to his comfortable shorts & a short shirt as usual & looked at Lisha sitting on the bed awaiting him to come out of the bathroom.

"What are you doing here?" he asked

"Awaiting my turn to change into my sleeping gear" she said & entered the bathroom - she didn't close the door behind her as usual - instead - she pulled a semi-transparent curtain.

"You still have a doubt that I'll run away?"

"Knowing you - Ya - I know that my safety is your prime concern & you're quite capable of running away for my sake."

"C'mon – Lisha - I just promised you that I won't run away from you - If I do run - I'll run away with you - No way, I'm going to leave you till the end..."

"Oh! That's nice to know" Lisha said with a bit of wile in her tone - even as she removed her dress & stood in her designer bikini.

"Hey! Close the door - I'm able to see almost everything" Chaits teased her.

"You've seen me in a similar wear when I wore that Charm Girl dress - so it doesn't matter now – but..." she pulled back the curtain half way - showing half of her body that donned a designer bikini, "The casino reminds me of an unfinished matter..."

"What unfinished matter?"

She came charging at him "What were your words? – oh – ya - you thought I was excited at the prospect of enjoying sex with you?"

"Lisha - I was just joking to take the tension out"

She came & stood square of him - well within touching distance - her navel directly in front of his eyes - he had to control a lot to take his eyes away from her exposed skin as he looked at her "And what was that? - your touch to my waist when we rode the bike was a friendly touch - eh?"

"I'll not lie to you - Lisha - I agree - It wasn't a friendly touch - it sprouted from my attraction toward you" he said lowering his eyes with shame, "I'm sorry for that..."

"The heck you are sorry about it" she said in seemingly angry tone - but there was something in her voice that told him - everything was alright - yet he doubted if his reading was wrong... "Look at me" she ordered & Chaits met her eyes with difficulty "now put your hands on my waist" he reluctantly did so "how's your touch different?"

"Look - Lisha - I did say I'm sorry for that"

"You'll have to touch me on my waist the way you did on the bike - till then - you can keep holding my waist - if you want to..."

Chaits looked at her stern expression & knew there was no way out - he'll have to touch her the way he had and accept what she'd punish him with... so he lowered his eyes back to her navel & ogled at her exposed skin - his feelings of lust for her rose as he looked more at her - his hands slowly started measuring the curves of her waist...

"Ohh! Chaits!" she moaned softly and slowly sat on his lap putting her arms around him - gone where were her flaming cheeks and the anger in her eyes "what have you done to me" she whispered, "I had planned to stay a soldier after my military training - I was a soldier till I met you - you've turned me into a woman - a woman who wants to be cared for - a woman who wants to be protected - a woman who wants you to touch her in love - I've been able to defy all my crushes - all those handsome men who tried their way to impress me - but with you - I've lost - all I want is - ummm..." she couldn't speak as she kissed him.

Chaits responded to her kiss - his heart pounding at this sudden turn of events...

"Kiss me, Chaits - I've never been kissed before - at this moment - I don't want to be a soldier. I just want to experience you - as a woman - I want to explore this newly found womanhood" she said amid shower of kisses. Chaits looked at her & found her eyes full of lust & want even as she unbuttoned his shirt "Let me be yours - completely"

This was too much for him & he put the idea of self-control away - his hands slowly moved over her naked skin & she audibly kept telling him feelings that surged through her - Chaits artistically explored her & she gave into his rhythm finally as he mounted her and let her know what exactly the term womanhood meant...

She kissed him as they lay side by side - trying to control their inflated breaths and he lovingly caressed her soft, beautiful long hair that spread across, covering his chest "Oh! What have you done to me, Chaits" she sighed happily as they passed off to sleep in each other's arms...

"Good morning - bed tea for you" Chaits opened his eyes to see her more beautiful than she'd looked before - he gladly sipped at it... It was a new feeling of love for Lisha & she did everything extra as possible to keep him happy - the day passed on happily in love.

"Lisha" Chaits said as his fingers run gently over hers as they sat next to each other after the dinner, remember - I said - I've a different plan for you..."

"Umm-hmm - what's the plan?"

"Close your eyes & sit here - I'll be back in a moment" he said & went into the bedroom - he returned with a small package - knelt down in front of her as he hid the packet behind him - gently, he held her hand, "now open your eyes"

She opened her eyes & saw him knelt down - smiling nervously...

"What?"

"Lisha - I've never been so serious in my life... all I want to say is" he gulped saliva in his nervousness, "all I want to say is - Marry me - be my wife" and he held the package and offered it to her...

Her heart beat fast as Chaits dramatically kissed the back of her hand - she kept the packet aside & sank on her knees beside him looked at him for a moment - put her arms around him & kissed her approval - she unwrapped the packet & heaved a long breath as she touched & unfolded the expensive oriental dress and looked at it...

# CHAPTER TWENTY-ONE

Next couple of days were the happiest as they passed them like a honeymoon couple in the forest - spending most of the time in love and trekking into the wild beautiful forest...

They were trekking in the forest "Chaits! I think - we're not alone. I think - I heard someone speak" They kept quiet & tried to listen for any human sound - all they could hear was the sound of birds. "Wait here - and don't make a sound." she whispered tiptoeing away & was soon out of sight - Chaits did what she'd asked him to do - wait silently & try and hear a human sound - but he wasn't able to - suddenly - he heard flutter of birds - it was Lisha who returned "They're here & looking for us" she whispered "we need to move immediately..." They tiptoed their way back as quickly as possible & started filling up their respective sacks - she drew the curtains packing every window & finally locked the door - she wiped off any dust that looked like a footstep & poured dust over as if it was by natural flow of wind...

"Where are we going?" he asked

"Away from here - anywhere..." she revved up the car & drove out of the garage, "Chaits, would you close & lock the garage, please"

She got down along with him - checking the tyres for any deflation while Chaits locked the garage ...

"Let's move" he said & sat in the car - three men stood in the drive way - blocking their path - he got out to face them - Lisha was behind the car checking the supplies she'd put in the boot - Chaits took few steps back & came next to her "They're here now - you hide for a moment as I tackle them & at the right moment start the car - I'll jump in..."

Lisha nodded & crouched as Chaits shut the boot as if he was alone & walked toward the driver's seat as if he would sit & drive off.

"Well-well - look - who do we have here?" one of them gleefully said in a loud voice "So you're hiding here while we search for you in KAL - great - but it's all over now." Chaits cautiously looked at them as they approached him...

"By the way - where's that sexy babe - sorry - let me rephrase - where are those sexy babes - the same ones who got away with you?

"I don't know"

"How did you manage that?"

"Well - if you can manage those girls with a price tag of up to 500 MYR - surely, with my wins in the casino - I'm sure - that kind of money will attract you as well." They looked at each other - greed in their eyes - but soon fear came upon their eyes...

"Nice try" one of them said, "you almost got us to agree - but there's something which is worth more than that... Our Life..." he said, "If we kill you - we get 5k each & we keep our life – that's the price tag you carry."

"And what if I manage to escape..."

"There are more than 200 guns waiting around this country - you need to think - 200+ guns - one aim - you..." he said in a sinister tone "You give us the USB & money - we'll let you go unharmed - in that case - you get 2 valuable days to escape this country from all the trouble & the danger..."

"How did you reach here?"

"Mr Wong is a clever man - he sent groups in each corner of Malaysia to hunt you out - most of them reported no sight of you - so he prepared a task force of 30 men & sent us to scout the jungle in your search - you've exactly 5 minutes to decide - others will be here - any moment & after that..."

Chaits thought for a moment I decided to call their bluff "I can give you 5OK - but I've been saying this all along that I don't know anything about a USB" he spoke while he came back to open the boot to show he was about to pay them 50K to them...

"How many people did you see?" he asked her in a low voice.

"About 20 - these were among them - they don't seem to be carrying guns."

He lifted a packet which was full of sandwiches prepared by Lisha & showed it to them, "Come - collect your 50K - forget about me & the USB that I've never seen..."

He kept the packet on top of the car & watched them greedily approach him - he waited for them till they were within his reach & suddenly attacked - 3 minutes - all of them lay knocked out...

"Look out" Lisha screamed even as he heard a swishing sound - he turned around & ducked - there were no guns - but they had short swords...

He quickly looked around & to his dismay roughly counted about 20 men - all armed with short swords - he dived into the ground as he avoided more thrusts at him & rolled around quickly. He picked up a stone as he got up & in one quick motion - threw it - the stone landed perfectly in the face of a person with such a force that he fell down unable to see anything... Chaits bent & picked up a sword - he knew he was not a swordsman - in fact - this was the first time he ever held one - he had learnt his skills with wooden sticks - his fighting instincts told him that he needed to use it to the perfection, its life - either his or theirs - he boosted himself...

One glance at the melee, & anyone could tell - Chaits didn't know how to wield a sword & was pitted against 20 odd men who seemed to be born with their swords.

There was a swishing sound & Chaits saw 7 of them go down - small daggers nailed deep in their chest - driven in by the force of impact into their chest - right up to the hilt - Chaits seized the opportunity & lashed the sword he held at an astounding speed at the man nearest to him - he managed to fatally wound about 2 of them as the men retreated a couple of steps in reflex - Lisha had suddenly jumped into the fray lifting a sword in each hand.

Chaits looked at her for a moment & realised - she's a master in her art of Kung Fu and shabbily attacked 2 men nearest to him. They were quick & Chaits realised that he was on back foot, he managed to fend the strikes well - but knew he'd lose this battle if he didn't think & act - soon...

Quickly, he looked around for a better weapon which he was comfortable with - his sight fell on a stout bamboo stick - about 5ft in length - he kicked a spool of dust in eyes of his opponents even as he saw 2 more running in to join them - he held the sword like a spear & threw it at the approaching men - it passed through chest of one - killing him instantly, even as Chaits bent down and lifted the stout stick.

He was very comfortable with the stick & began whirling it at a high speed - the speed was so much that the men who had swords just could just circle around him waiting their chance to pounce upon him - one of them finally dared to put his sword at the stick - the impact was such that the sword fell off his hand, the though stick broke into 2 equal pieces ... Now he held 2 equal length - not so short, stout sticks & wielded them with equal vigour & speed...

The men who had swords had no chance the way he wielded his sticks - Chaits soon put them on back foot.

Lisha had by now killed all her opponents & looked at Chaits who was beating the hell out of his opponents with his sticks - finally all the swords lay on the ground & his opponents rubbed their swollen arms in pain - yelping out every time his stick made a contact. Lisha joined him cutting off their retreat from the back - the guys knew that they were trapped between Chaits & Lisha - they looked at each other & begged for mercy - Chaits stopped hitting them with his sticks as he considered letting them go for a moment - in one quick movement they put their hand in their pockets. & brought out a capsule - Chaits hit out in reflex but was late - he could knock a capsule off from only one - the others chewed their capsules & lay dead at his feet...

"Enough of this hide & seek game!" he thundered at the only one alive and he viciously hit his stick on his shoulder bone - the man whined in pain, "now - if you don't want any further pain - you talk - or I can keep hitting you like this..."

The man's eyes showed fear of extreme degree - he looked at Chaits whose eyes showed no mercy at all..."Who are you working for?"

"Mr Wong - he owns the new casino."

"What's the USB all about?"

His eyes now showed terror as he shut up only to open his mouth to scream in agony. Chaits hit a vicious blow with his stick on the shin "He'll kill me if I tell you more!"

"I'll kill you if you don't tell me about it - I'm sure he'll just get you killed with ease - but - I'll keep hitting you with this stick harder & harder - you'll feel pain - more pain - as the bones in your body break - till you die - it's your choice..." and Chaits left the words hanging on him...

He looked at Chaits - his eyes filled with terror - his heart left with no hope "I'll talk..." he said finally as he looked at Lisha pull her daggers out of the men & coolly wipe the blood on their clothes & put them back in her dagger holster...

"So you were about to enlighten me about the USB that I don't have & wanted to kill me for not having it..." Chaits prodded him

"I don't know much - but from what I heard - Mr Wong has some sort of agreement with the terrorists who operate worldwide - I think they are planning big attacks - world wide - Malaysia included - we are just the tough recovery guys from the casino..."

Lisha looked at the man not ready to digest the information he had divulged.

"But you came to kill me for that USB - this means you're a terrorist as well."

"I'm not a terrorist."

"Why didn't you go to the police when you have so much information..."

"We can't - they'll kill us - just as they killed the owner & made his son accept the terms."

"You still didn't tell me what's in the USB that you're looking for..." Chaits knew that sooner or later Lisha would guess that he already knew what that USB contained so he kept on asking. It's better if she thinks they share the same information...

"I think that USB may contain a master plan of their terrorist attacks that they'd be carrying out in various cites of the world."

"Oh! That's ridiculous!" said Lisha

"Do you know which cities?"

"No - I only know that USB may have that information - today - you're lucky - we found you - that's the reason you're alive & I'm talking..." he said ruefully.

"What do you mean?" Lisha asked

"Maybe in few days you'll face them - the real terrorists - they have guns - not swords & they're much more ruthless - you can only threaten me to break my bones - but - believe me - they'd do exactly that if they catch you."

"Now that I know who's my enemy is - I'll be ready for that..." Chaits said in a dangerous tone.

"And you better leave him right now" he said looking at Lisha, "nobody knows who you are. If they capture you along with him - only God Almighty can save you - they'll rape you till death."

"Shut up!" Lisha said & made a small cut on his arm with the sword she still held - they both were off guard for a moment as they digested what the man said - he took his chance & rolled off, grabbed a sword that lay next to him. With a fixed look of decision - stabbed his heart with it...

"Chaits! Those guys must really be dangerous - this man just committed Hara-Kiri from the fear to face them." Lisha said with concern.

"Excuse me" Chaits said & hid behind a tree & threw up his stomach.

"Chaits! Are you alright?"

"Yes" he gasped for breath as he threw up again, "it's just that I've never been in a bloodbath - but - I think I'll have to get used to it now..."

She kept rubbing his back vigorously till he could throw up no more. They sat in the car without a further word as they drove away...

## CHAPTER TWENTY-TWO

"Where are we going?"

"To be precise - not yet decided."

"How long will we run like this?"

"Till the time you get out & Malaysia or till such time - they kill me." Lisha said firmly.

"You don't have to be in this anymore!" Chaits said musing, "one thing's certain - they're going to find me & kill me - just because in good faith as a human - I tried to help a fellow passenger - you've nothing to do with this..."

"I agree with you - I've nothing to do with this..."Lisha said pulling the car to a side as she stopped, "I also agree that I've nothing to do with them - but, I've got everything to do with you - remember you asked me to marry you & I accepted - and marriage means - Till Death Do Us Part... When you walk, I will be your shadow... When you stop, I will be your destination..." Lisha said this holding his hand "so - let's live to marry - or both die - obviously - me first - they'll not reach you till I'm alive - so shut up! & put your nonsense aside - I'm sure - we'll win in this battle." They sat holding hands, thinking hard for the best of plans which could work...

Lisha came to a decision - she revved up the car & off they were "We are going to the forest in Penang" she said "they have a better chance of finding us if we go to towns or cities - gimme another 5000 MYR. I need to arrange few things..."

They drove using internal roads & lanes and stopped at various places for Lisha to collect the things. She bought what wanted - It was about 3 AM in the morning when she parked her car in the garage of a similar farm house in a forest of Penang... "Chaits" she said huffing & puffing "you need to help me with this" she said trying to lift a heavy canvass bag - together - they somehow managed to get the bag inside...

"My God! Lisha! What's this stuff... It's so heavy." Chaits asked - he'd been sitting in the car all the time to avoid detection while she purchased what she wanted.

"These are our food supplies for a month" she said as she removed a big carton of canned food "and the rest are tools - we may need for our protection & as well few weapons for us to fight for our survival."

Though tired, she managed to boil a readymade pack which they gobbled cup - Chaits lay on the bed - unable to sleep - she snuggled up next to him & put a loving arm around him...

"Don't you want to change in your sleeping gear?" she asked pecking his cheek in affection.

"Lisha" he said not responding to her affection "I'm sorry to have thrown up the way I did - I'm not used to looking at blood & here - I've killed few people. I'm a murderer..."

"Stop brooding - Chaits" she said with a firm voice, "the act was totally in self-defence - had you not killed them, they'd have killed you - and those who you killed were not humans - they were terrorists & they would keep killing good people - thousands of innocent people. If you don't do it - the lives of those thousands of innocent lives will remain on your conscience - just think this way - you couldn't run away leaving innocent Laila - she was only one person - imagine how you'll feel if you know that several hundred people died - just because you preferred not to kill few terrorists who were at your mercy - I know you - you'll never be able to meet your own eyes when you look into the mirror if that happens..."

"This is not my job - this job belongs to police or military - why can't we go to police & tell them everything we know?"

"I thought about it - it won't work till we have proof - Mr Wong seems to have connections in high places - nothing may happen to him - but we may get exposed like sitting ducks for those terrorists & die without a fight - yes, if we do get a proof - that's the first thing we're going to do..."

Chaits thought for a moment - the loving caresses of Lisha soothed him and he was soon uncomfortably asleep - nightmares of blood hounding him... He felt better when he woke up the next day though he was still sore with the thought of killing those men - he reached out but Lisha was not there - he looked into the kitchen - tea was ready, the food was cooked but no sign of Lisha... 'She must have gone to get something' he thought & sipped at the tea wondering what a simple pleasure trip had turned into - a blood bath! He heard a faint tapping noise somewhere outside the house & his senses alerted him - he looked around & found a stout stick - he slowly opened the main door & stealthily approached this tapping sound that seemed like someone hammering a nail - the sound was intermittent. He hid in the trees waiting the sound to start again - the sound came directly over his head & he looked up...

"Lisha! What are you doing up on tree?"

She slithered down the tree & smiled, "Good morning", she said as she collected a bundle of wire, "I'm putting up some lights that I can switch ON if I feel we're in danger - it's very dark around at night - this will not only light up the entire area around the house for us to see clearly - but, also blind those who approach..."

"Here, let me help you" said Chaits & within an hour's time, the lights were set up. Then, they proceeded with a wire which they fenced about few inches from the ground. It was almost invisible & sure to trip anyone who walked toward the house - once finished they sat down to lunch...

"You seem to be very good with the sticks - where did you learn that?"

"Well" Chaits was a bit pleased with this praise after he'd seen Lisha fight & finish off many more terrorists than him "Actually, I learnt it for a ritual - every year on a particular auspicious day - we go to our village to offer prayers to our family deity - it's a huge carnival. The idol of the deity is taken out in a long procession with different troupes displaying various talents - I love that. So I started learning it. I first learnt to wield a long stick - then graduated to use 2 short sticks like swords - next year I'll be in the league to learn with an actual sword – oh! How I wish I'd have already learnt that already..."

"In fact - you're very good at it - I want to learn it. Will you teach me?"

"Lisha - even the girls display these arts in the procession - and as my wife - I'd love if you can do that..."

"Follow me" she said & she collected 2 stout sticks amongst many that were stored there "hold this stick not like this, this way – horizontally." she said when they came out on the lawn - she rushed into the house & returned with a sword - with one quick movement - her sword came down on the centre of the stick that he held - he didn't even feet a jerk of impact as the sword neatly cut the stick into halves...

"Wow - Lisha - this stuff is amazing"

She did exactly the same with the second stick & held up the 2 short sticks, "C'mon" she yelled & attacked him - in about 5 minutes - she realised his talent & his speed with the sticks. The sticks she held - they were no longer in her hands they were flying off... "This is fantastic Chaits!" she screamed in joy, "you can wield swords better than me - the only thing that keeps you is your fear of hurting someone - I'm sure you'll be able to do the same with swords."

"You're right Lisha - I'm not used to spilling blood - maybe that's the reason I wasn't able to use the sword - but I've a question - didn't you feel any remorse when you killed those terrorists?"

"No - none at all - you forget I've had my military training - it was not in the school. We were trained in the military camps by real soldiers & we did carry out real missions - especially, against the ruthless drug dealers."

"Wow! You mean real military action?"

"Ya - the first time I saw someone getting killed was my friend who got hit by a bullet - I did throw up worse than you did. It took me about a week to overcome that ghastly thing - but then, I'd made up my mind to kill all those bastards & then I feel nothing about it - you see - that's why, I'm a soldier - I only know how to protect my people - even if it means killing a lot of bad guys." Chaits looked at her - stunned by her confession, then slowly put his hand over her shoulder as he pulled her toward him - she clung to him weeping, "I'd applied to join the military forces here & I know - I'm shortlisted - Chaits, please let me remain a soldier - whenever I'm with you - I become a woman & not remain a soldier..."

Chaits slowly patted her to comfort her - as he led her toward the house & made her sit on the sofa as he delicately wiped off her flowing tears. "I promise..." he said softly, "I'll not force you to be a woman - you can make your choice - and I also promise - I'll still love you - irrespective of your decision."

"Oh! Chaits ... this goodness of your heart & your unflinching love for me - makes me go weak & wants me to be a woman." she said & hugged him as she wept uncontrolled...

The balance day passed as he tried consoling her. He tried doing lot of tricks & put up his charming best to get her melancholy off her mind but to no avail - finally he could think of nothing else, 'Let her sleep it off. That should make her feel better...' he took a cold shower to ease his mind & came back she was still sitting on the sofa brooding.

"Lisha" he said trying to comfort her, "go to sleep that should allow you to rest your mind & you'll feel good when you wake up tomorrow" he held her hand & led her to bed, "try sleeping it off." he said as he caressed her back in concern to comfort her - she kept on looking at him without a blink - lost in some thought - deep inside her mind...

"I'd like to take a cool shower" she said suddenly getting up & ran into the bathroom even before he could react. Maybe that'll cool her off he thought as he stretched on the bed - he closed his eyes as his mind furiously thought about how he could possibly bring the smile on her face - he lay thus & didn't open his eyes when he heard Lisha come out of the bathroom, 'Let her be herself' he thought... He was feeling almost sleepy now - he could smell freshness of her body as she lay next to him after the cool shower - he could smell the feminine scent of her shampoo & her perfume. He wanted to put an arm around her - but controlled...

All his sleep vanished when he felt her fingers unbuttoning his shirt & her lips furiously kissing his bare chest - he opened his eyes to look at Lisha who seemed to be full of lust for him. His hand started gently running through her soft & silky long hair & soon touched her bare back...

"I thought about it Chaits" she said amid her lusty display of kisses & the flicks of her tongue as she licked at him, "I thought really hard, and I now know - I want to be a normal woman & live my life with you - someone else can take my place as a soldier - I don't want to lose you..."

Chaits slowly moved his hands & gently started exploring her need of quenching her lust for him - he soon realised that her actions of lust sprouted through her love for him and she started responding to his touches - he held her & kissed her as his hands re-explored her perfectly carved out figure - soon they gave in to their lust for each other & regaled in their feelings to be with each other - she was no longer a soldier - she was Lisha - Lisha who was in love with him - Lisha who yearned for his tender touch - Lisha who wanted to settle down in matrimony with him - Till Death Parted them...

## CHAPTER TWENTY-THREE

They woke up - happy for the decision they had taken as they thought about only one thing which was the need - Escape from Malaysia, away from those terrorists.

"This is it!" Lisha exclaimed in joy as if she was Archimedes and about to shout Eureka! "Chaits, I've a solution to our problem - I am in tourism - I know of a cruise that's moving off Penang. It will head first to Singapore - we'll board that cruise to Singapore - never to return - once in Singapore - we split - you fly back to Mumbai & get the paperwork for our wedding ready & I go to my home in Philippines, to my people & join you at our wedding..."

"But - will those terrorists we met in Penang not keep a lookout?"

"Don't worry about that. The captain of the cruise is my friend - I'll ask him to wait on the border of international water in the sea - Kaz Chan has fishermen friends - they'll smuggle us out on their fishing trawler & take us to the cruise..."

Chaits had a smile on his face. He knew if something has to work - this is their only chance... "So - when do we leave for Penang?"

"We are in the thick jungle within Penang. It's hardly about an hour's drive from here."

"Great - go ahead & we will get this arranged" he said putting his arm around her," the sooner the better - I definitely need a good wife - it's urgent for my life."

She put her arms around him jumped as he lifted her & walked across to the bedroom still carrying her in his arms & gently laid her on the bed. They forgot the time as their feelings took their action over...

They were up & ready early in the noon after the lunch. Lisha drove at her best speed and soon parked the car in the huge parking lot - like a magician - she brought out a straw hat & gave it to Chaits – "Wear this all the time & don't get out of the car" she said handing over a pack of cigarettes, "smoke yourself to glory if you want - but don't get out of the car. It'll take me about an hour or so." she pecked him on his cheek to cheer him up & briskly walked into the mall...

Chaits sat down pulling the hat low over his forehead & tried to catch the action on the road & in the parking - he was amid crowd after a long time. He lit up a cigarette & dragged it deep into his lungs who thanked him for quenching their thirst for a smoke - he sat there watching all the activity around. Then he looked at the list of shops in the mall - he couldn't control himself - he got out of the car still keeping the hat low over his forehead to avoid recognition & checked his image on the closed window - it'll be difficult for anyone to recognise him... He had kept most of his cash at the forest home but had enough on him - he checked few shops out before he entered one - he took out a small chit & pointed at a display "I want this one - in this size."

"This'll cost you 11,500 MYR, Sir" the girl said smiling - her eyes wide with the expression that Chaits knew - Impressed by Him.

"Good" he said matching it carefully, "please pack it" and he looked at his watch - 15 more minutes at least & returned to the car – Oops! The car was locked - he didn't realize that he would need the keys to open it... 'Well-well' he thought, 'Madame Lisha is going to be angry seeing me standing outside the car..." He removed the hat & wiped off the sweat that formed - it really was a hot day... He put his bag containing his purchases on the bonnet of Lisha's car & looked at the items again - he put a small item in his pocket & smiled - he was lost in some day dream...

He came back to his senses when he felt a hard rod push him from behind "Don't make a move - do exactly as I tell you" a raspy voice said in a low voice.

Chaits instantly realised his mistake - he should've sat still in the car - he hoped that Lisha wasn't around 'At least - let her be safe.' he thought.

"Move" the raspy voice ordered & prodded the way they needed him to walk.

Lisha's heart was beating fast. She had anticipated the work & bookings to be over in about 45 minutes - it was almost an hour now... 'I hope Chaits is safe - I shouldn't have brought him along' she thought she smiled as the counter girl handed her the packet with all the required paperwork & their travel tickets, 'Good' Lisha thought, 'if everything goes right - the way I planned - Chaits should reach Mumbal in next 3-4 days & I'll be with Lin around same time - what would her reaction be when I tell her that we're getting married?' she was absorbed in her thoughts as she walked into the parking lot - she looked at a small bag on her bonnet & wondered who'd left it - perhaps - he'd know...

She looked into the car through the windshield to see what Chaits was doing - her heart skipped a beat - he was missing - she opened the packet & looked at the contents - she instantly realised that this was his stuff - it lay over the bag which contained his roller skates - she held those in her hand as her eyes wildly looked around for any sign - to her dismay - she saw Chaits - he was forcibly being pushed into a car - his height & his straw hat made it easy for her to recognise him...

"Shit" she muttered to herself as she unlocked the car & furiously drove out of the parking lot - she kept a safe distance as she followed the car - they were going toward the hill behind the Kek Lok Si Temple - the same hill where terrorists had chased them on his roller skates - once they left the junction - the road was a bit lonely & she had to increase the distance between the two cars.

'Obviously - they still don't know me - nor they recognize this car - else they would have waited for my return as well - why did you have to get out of the car, Chaits?' she kept on muttering as she followed the car about a turn or so behind - she saw the car take a left turn - now going downhill - after a short distance - the car took a right turn & Lisha stopped - she knew this road - it was a dead end. The end of that road was a cold storage & warehouse belonging to a fishing company...

She picked up her mobile & dialled the directory services - "Mr Wong" the voice on other end confirmed - and she sadly shook her head - finally Wong had managed to capture him - she looked at the road & instantly knew that the warehouse was strategically built - any vehicle that passed downhill could be seen easily though the warehouse was about 3kms away - there was nothing to obstruct the view - there was no other road that led there - Chaits was trapped - they'll definitely kill him if they see any unknown vehicle approach - she didn't take that turn but drove on -

she'll have to return by the dusk & walk it out 'I hope they don't kill him before I reach there.'

She parked at a road side motel & opened the boot of her car - deftly she gathered the weapons she'd need & placed the balance back - she looked at her watch - every second that passed seemed like eon to her 'I hope he's safe - and if they kill him - they'll pay the price - heavily.' She hoped & vowed in the same breath...

She started the car as the Sun began to down, throwing up golden shades with tint of reddish–orange - she turned off the headlights & drove with parking lights & then turned off all the lights as she approached the turn - she saw a small gutter like ditch to a side & carefully drove & parked her car as if some driver had misjudged the turn & hit the side. She turned on the hazard lights as a normal driver would do & proceeded on foot crisscrossing her path. She walked down the hill - fleet footed as a lamb. She wore a black jacket that held her weapons for her as well made it difficult to be seen in the dark.

The cross country walk was a short distance. She hid behind the nearest tree as she carefully watched the warehouse - she was crouching real low to avoid the high beam of a car that approached the warehouse...

"Good evening, Mr Wong" the guard shouted his salute. Lisha could clearly hear them. She was that close to the warehouse...

"Everything ok?"

"Yes - sir - no bird spotted around"

"Good" & the car entered the warehouse & parked. The light from the headlights of the car was enough for Lisha to get the perfect view of the guard around the building - she stealthily circled around to see more of it, 'God! This place seems to be full of terrorists. There must be at least

50-60, maybe, almost same number in the what looks like a residential building next to the main building...' she carefully watched the guards pace up & down & calculated the time mentally - she sprinted across to the tree nearest to the high fence, 'I hope this fence is not wired' she hopefully wished & looked around...

She saw a cat on prowl next to her, 'I know it's wrong to hurt animals - but for him - I'm ready to break any rule' she thought & quickly grabbed it flinging it at the fence - the fence was wired - not with electrical current but with intruder alarm which blared & blinding lights turned on - the poor cat's hind leg was entangled in a wire as it tried desperately to release itself.

"What's the racket about?" one asked as he looked around.

"It's this damned cat - it seems she tried breaking in" the guard answered him.

"See if you can release it - if you can't then that's your dinner. I don't want this alarm to go off again for wrong reasons - Mr Wong is inside the warehouse. I'll turn off the alarm system till you get rid of that cat" & he walked away.

Lisha took her chance as a couple of them tried releasing the cat. The lights had been switched off along with the alarm - she quickly scouted toward the fence & touched it - No Alarm...

She stood parallel to a fence post to make it difficult for anyone to see her. She took 2-3 quick steps backward & ran and heaved up using the spaces in the fence as footholds & jumped over it - she landed light footed as a cat would & rolled off in to the dark shadow next to the wall - she opened the package she had tied to her back & put on her dagger holster which held about a dozen of them - put on the other one which held her swords - the jacket housed her other small weaponry.

She carefully peeped out of the shadow to see a guard walk toward her on his round - she quietly tiptoed behind him - the guy froze as she stuck a needle on his neck - freezing a particular nerve - he stood as if he was a statue - she dragged him into the shadows & he lay there still - he'd have to wait till someone removed the needle... She followed the suit till every guard outside the main building was frozen - now she scouted around to check for an opening - getting in through the main door could prove fatal...

'Chaits! Please make a sound - I need to know that you're alive & the place they've kept you' she desperately wanted to hear his voice - her heart was already sinking with the thought of him being dead... 'If they've killed him - I promise - nobody shall leave this place alive' she vowed in her anger.

She saw a light that showed an open window on the $2^{nd}$ storey as it lit up. She saw a water pipe next to it - that stretched right from the ground to the terrace - she grabbed at it & heaved herself & climbed up the 2 storeys faster than a monkey would... She groped around & peeped inside as soon as she got a firm foothold...

Lisha saw a group of terrorists - they all held swords – no guns. 'That is strange' she thought, 'the guy warned us guns before committing Hara-Kiri - but these terrorists have no guns, maybe the others in this building do...'

She hid behind the curtain - still hanging half outside the window - Wong finished his briefing. In another 15 minutes he explained - how the terrorists will wreath havoc in which city & how they'd start their travel in next 10 days... They started to leave & Lisha eased inside the window behind the curtain.

"Mr Wong, if this data is on a USB - surely this can be read over by email - why USB?"

"Dear brother Kasim, the email stuff is volatile - I own a group of 50 hackers who easily hack into other accounts - I'm sure, our enemies too have a group of hackers - that's unsafe - USB contains data that's available only to the person using it, so hold your horse - if Cynthia says 3 days are enough for him to talk - be sure - she's capable of it..." and they walked out. The guards put the lights off & shut the door behind them.

Lisha tiptoed toward the door, 'He's alive - have to find him before they start hurting him' she carefully peeped out - all clear... she made her way to the iron platform in search for him. Finding Chaits was a priority - she looked at the layout the structure. The aisle she stood on was made of iron platform - edge to edge in C shape - the same was the layout for the first storey & the centre was open to all the storeys - one could easily see what was the action there. She looked over the railing – at least 25 people guarded the entrance - all armed with swords.

She saw Wong exit toward the back where the cove was & judged that there would be another structure which would house a line of cold storages - all the fish they caught would be stored there. She looked over the railing again & saw Cynthia walk up the iron stairway - making a wishful tick-tock sound as she walked - she turned to her left toward the other side & opened the door. Lisha's joy knew no bounds as her sight fell on Chaits who was tied to a chair - he looked blankly at Cynthia as she entered the room - she kept a box she carried on a stool in front of him, walked out of the room & leaned over the railing. She clapped to get attention of people guarding the main entrance "You're about to hear sweet music, the Indian spy's going to sing it for us - so do enjoy yourselves" the guards clapped in glee. Lisha was wondering what she meant…

She looked around - the iron aisles enabled people to different rooms were constructed in C shape - there were 3 stairs that led downward from every wall of the C shaped structure - Chaits was on the opposite - she saw 2 doors open on the 2$^{nd}$ floor & she didn't know how many on 1$^{st}$ landing…

She tiptoed her way to the first open door & cautiously peeked in 3 people, they were watching football on the TV - she stepped in a closed the door - she opened the door after about a minute - her sword dripping blood from dead men inside the room - she followed the pattern with the second room - she quickly covered the path to the stairs that were nearest to the room where Chaits was bound to the chair…

"You know - you are the most handsome Lover boy - I've ever seen or met" Lisha was now able to clearly hear Cynthia's voice, "It's a pity that you're an Indian spy & I'll have to work torture on you - but, to think of it, I'll certainly love to work sex on you - why are you such an idiot?" she continued in a jovial tone, "You know that anyways we'll kill you - but I like you - you're such a sweet Lover boy - I'll give you options - 1) You join us - give us the USB and work for our goals in India - and your reward is - lots of money - and lots of love making with me…

Cynthia made the 1$^{st}$ offer - Lisha hoped that Chaits would say something to keep Cynthia occupied even as she crept her way on the railings to the landing below - she saw a light in other rooms & entered those rooms – '15 down - don't know - how many more yet' & she tiptoed her way back to the room where Chaits was & peeked in - Cynthia had a sword in her hand and she stood close to Chaits - Lisha couldn't risk an ambush at Cynthia - Cynthia might kill Chaits in reflex - so she stood there peeping in - waiting for her chance to enter...

"Your time's up" Cynthia said as she put the sword to Chaits throat & removed the two top buttons off his shirt "Now - for my next option 2) Either, accept my first offer & live - or - give me the USB & die - an easy death... No pain - No gain... head sliced off within seconds... You've time to consider till I remove every button on your shirt" she slowly kept on removing the buttons - one by one...

'C'mon - move away from him' Lisha wished...

"Oh! Oohhh!" Cynthia faked a sensuous moan; "you do have a sexy build, Oh! What a waste - wouldn't you like to know what's the third option - sweetheart?"

She sensuously moved her hand on his chest - slowly following it with kisses & licking her kisses... "Consider this is a kind of crazy love - you've exactly 10 seconds to accept - or my 3$^{rd}$ option will be Pain - Full of Love..."

Chaits screamed in pain as Cynthia pricked his chest with a needle - his scream was cut short as she kissed him on the lips - covering and stifling his scream...

"See - this is what is known as Pain of Love" she said & followed the suit by pricking another needle about an inch away... and kissing him...

"You - horny bitch" in pain, Chaits swore at her as she laughed wickedly...

"This is just a start - sweetheart - I'm going to carry on till I prick every inch of your body then let you feel the pain - overnight - tomorrow morning - I follow up - I remove these needles - one by one - I won't let you scream in pain - because every time you open your mouth to scream - I'll kiss you - lovingly." she pricked in the third needle & kissed him as his mouth opened to scream, "After this" she continued in a sinister tone, "you'll either yield or I repeat... The difference will be - these needles will be red hot - I'll give you exactly a minute to think..."

Chaits desperately thought - but the pain increased as she tickled the needles with flicks of her tongue. He could see no mercy in her lusty eyes - he knew that by talking to her he could prolong the torture but not avoid it - he definitely was not going to turn in the plan of terrorism - he preferred a painful death...

"Alright, Cynthia - I agree that you're a master in this art of torture & I know that this'll finally end with my death" he said still gasping in pain, "but, don't you think that I've a right to know why am I being tortured & killed - what's in a small USB? I can buy hundreds of those & gift them to you..." he stopped as she slapped him hard...

"Still want to play games?" she teased him by running a loving finger on his swollen cheek.

"No - I just want to be sure before I settle down on one of your options - and that's the reason I must know who you are working for - what are your plans & what'll I gain in the end..."

"Now - you're talking sweetheart," she said with a fake excitement, "here let me kiss you for a fresh start" she pricked another needle as she kissed him - stifling his scream "Ok - here's the deal - all these years the governments around the world are run by few selfish people who only know to plunder & loot the common people - there are various groups in each country who are fighting to get rid of these bastards."

Chaits looked at her in wonder & then away from her toward the door - his heart skipped a beat as he saw Lisha peek in keeping a finger on her lips, signalling him to carry on - he looked back at Cynthia "That's a stale news - where do you come in?"

"I belong to a similar group that's based in Europe - we realised that we cannot fight these governments in our small groups - further these bastards branded us as terrorists & started killing our people. So, we - the so called terrorist groups - all over the world, joined hands - we realised that when two countries wage war - weakens their defence & depletes their armies – Iraq, Lebanon and Syria are wonderful examples - so - we have devised attacks on major cities around the globe. We've taken care to see that when we carry out these attacks - each country will blame its rival country. These will be relentless attacks - one after the other - till these countries wage war against each other... and when they do - that's our chance to stronghold our establishment - all over the globe. One day - we'll win & rule - the common man will rule..."

"You're insane..." Chaits said exasperated as their plan unfolded - so did the data in the USB.

"We're not insane - we're not terrorists - we're modern revolutionaries" she said vehemently, "and sweetheart - you can be one of us - when we win & start ruling - I'll marry you & you'll be my king - I know I can persuade Wong to spare your life."

"And, what if I don't?"

"You'll die & the victory still will be ours. The USB you possess has the master plan for these attacks. If you die without letting us know - we still will be able to duplicate the master plan - the only thing that will change is the schedule of action - why do you want to give up life when you can enjoy it with me?"

"And how do you attack?"

"We've trained many groups in structure demolition - they will demolish many business centres around the world

& with it - the governments would lose the businesses & the people who get the business for them..."

"Aren't thousands of common people who work there - get the business for them?"

"The number of common people who die in these attacks would be honoured as martyrs - their death will dissuade others from working - we'll achieve our goal..." she got up from his lap & walked across to the intercom, "connect me to Mr Wong" she commanded - even as Chaits shook his head at the insanity of their purpose...

"Mr.Wong - good news - he's opened up - it took only 3-4 pricks to get him to talk - he doesn't seem to be trained for torture. I'll suggest - he lives in our custody - I'll persuade him to join us, what? - well, if he turns a traitor, I'll be the first one to put a bullet through him." Lisha slipped quietly into the room & shut the door without a noise even as Cynthia spoke to Wong.

Cynthia turned around & looked startled at Lisha who'd crept in & gave a vicious smile "Oh! So this wild cat is love with you" she looked at Lisha & extended her arm that held the sword, "how about a fair cat fight?" she said as she dropped her sword to the ground - Lisha looked at her & threw her sword down as well put her other gear that held her smaller weaponry down & threw a dagger that stuck to Chaits' chair.

"Don't do this Lisha" Chaits warned her.

"Don't worry" she said & took a classic Kung Fu pose, "Hhaaaahh!"

The room was big enough for them to fight & they started circling each other, poised for lethal attack - Cynthia made the first move as she spun around flashing a deadly kick which Lisha ducked & countered by spinning around in crouched position extending her right leg which

Cynthia avoided by jumping over it... They lashed out their arms & feet at each other for few moments & evaded successfully, both unable to connect before they stopped & circled around again. Then they lashed out at each other - this time positioning themselves within striking distance of each other - Chaits watched them a bit concerned for Lisha - he had experienced the muscular tall body of Cynthia...

His face lit up when he saw Lisha getting an upper hand in the duel - Lisha suddenly struck a strong kick in Cynthia's abdomen sending her reeling backward to the wall - she took this opportunity & rushed to Chaits & cut off the ropes that bound his hand with the dagger she'd thrown, stuck to his chair.

"Lisha! Look out!" Chaits cautioned her as Cynthia recovered - she gave the dagger to Chaits & turned back to ward off a blow from Cynthia - Chaits watched the duel as he started cutting off the balance ropes that tied him - Cynthia was wild with fury & was hitting out at Lisha dangerously - Chaits freed himself off the ropes that bound him & screamed as he removed the needles that were pricked deep in his body - Lisha couldn't concentrate hearing his screams & looked back at him - Cynthia took her chance, lifted Lisha & threw her - she hit the ground - a bit stunned & slid toward Chaits even as he got off the chair. He caught her in time to avoid her hitting the stool...

"You - ok?" he asked.

"Ya" Lisha said looking at Cynthia who stood there in shorts & a short blouse - proudly displaying her well-toned body & muscles - a wicked smile curled on her lips as she pointed at both - jeering them by a thumbs-down sign. She approached them even as Lisha recovered - Chaits pushed Lisha to one side. Lisha cautioned him...

Cynthia stood within arm's distance from Chaits & displayed her powerful body again "Tch Tch - I'll hate hurting you - Lover boy" she said & lashed out an ugly fist at him - he simply stopped it with his palm & looked at her & waived a finger of caution - she tossed her hair in style brushing off his caution & smiled. She lashed out with her free hand - Chaits was quick to duck it in reflex & hit out a fierce box on her face - the impact was such that Cynthia stood straight & still... slowly she tilted backward falling with a huge thud... knocked out.

"Let's cage this wild cat before she regains" Chaits said moving her from the floor & making her sit on the same chair & tied her exactly the way he was tied while Lisha collected her gear.

"Here, Chaits - I got these metal batons for you to protect yourself - I know you are fantastic in using sticks of this size."

Chaits took those & swished them around a bit, "They're light as sticks"

"Let's go there are many more waiting down - ready to greet us with swords " Lisha pulled his hand & started moving but stopped and turned around - she gagged Cynthia's mouth even as she regained consciousness & slapped her so that she regained complete consciousness, "There - this will keep you from warning others - see the tables turn?" Lisha spoke, her voice full of aggression, "now - hear this - Yes - I Love him - I may not worry if you torture me - but you made a mistake - he's not a spy - to let you know how it feels..."she took handful of Cynthia's special torture needles pricked them into her body. Chaits could sense her screams that poured out of her expressions - while with her gags her screams could be heard faintly...

"C'mon, Lisha - don't do it - there's a difference between you & her. Let her know that good people don't torture their victims" he said pulling Lisha away from Cynthia - Cynthia's eyes showed unfathomable hate for Lisha... Lisha picked up her blood stained sword & slowly pushed the door open & peeped out. Chaits followed her out. Cynthia struggled to get out of the ropes.

Lisha tiptoed to the central stairs & waived to Chaits to back her up from the other staircase they both started climbing down, matching each other's stealthy steps & Lisha suddenly got on the railing & slid down to the centre of the hall...

There was an astonished yell in the hall as the guards looked at Lisha & rushed at her - Chaits ran down the balance stairs to help Lisha who was surrounded by 20-25 guards. For few minutes there was only sound of clangs as metals struck at each other - an occasional scream of people getting fatal wounds echoed then there was silence...

Chaits & Lisha stood gasping for breath surrounded by bodies of dead guards - not a single guard lived - more guards rushed in from the landings & another fight ensued - within minutes the room looked like excavated graveyard as Lisha & Chaits rushed to the main door to escape... Lisha opened the main door & quickly shut it back bolting it from inside...

"Chaits there are about hundred more out there" she screamed, even as fearful blows fell on the main door. The guards outside started their efforts to break down the main door - they ran toward the exit where Lisha had seen Wong disappear...

They opened the door & looked at many rows of smaller cabins with high quality doors which were shut airtight - they shut & bolted the door behind them...

"This isn't cold for a cold storage" Chaits said & sniffed, "I don't smell the fish either."

"This is the main room where the cold storages are located you idiot - keep quiet - I'd first like to find if there's any guard lurking around..."

Chaits obeyed & they took to two flanks that ran throughout the storage room dividing the entire storage into 3 parts. They quickly scouted the entire corridor - there was nobody around - Lisha started toward the main rear exit and stopped - Chaits was not with her... she turned around in alarm - she saw him struggling to open the door of one of the cold storages - perplexed & annoyed at his behaviour she rushed back to him.

"What the hell are you doing?" she asked

"I've never seen fish stored in a cold storage - so was just checking out how that's done."

"This is no time to do that..." she started even as Chaits managed to pry open the door & looked at the open cold storage, mouth equally wide open...

Chaits looked at her expression & turned around "What kind of fireworks are these?" he said lifting one of the things.

"Keep it there Chaits - don't touch it - these are highly dangerous, high intensity explosives - the one that you hold in your hand can demolish this entire storage along with us."

"I've seen a lot of smaller versions of these in India at festival called Diwali - even children light these up with ease."

She looked at the main door to the storage they had entered. There was no banging sound yet which clearly meant the guards were still trying to break the main door...

"Chaits," she said in an urgent voice, "I think, we have time enough to check these cold vaults - I want you to stay here & keep a watch on the rear door - I'm going to check this place out." she said & left - she opened the vaults one by one & made exasperated sounds as she looked at the firearms and the stuff stored in there...

Chaits looked at the vault opened by him - he saw a plastic box which contained slow burning fuses - he pulled the box & started playing with them. He tied knots & laced them elongating them. He must have tied the entire bundle while Lisha checked the vaults out - she returned with lots of things packed in her spare bag - she also held an ugly looking gun "C'mon - let's move" she said with urgency, "and I told you not to play with that..."

"Don't worry" Chaits asserted her as he attached his entire laced work to an explosive stick in the centre "I know how to play safe with these though I wonder how long does it take to burn one fuse."

"These are Chinese make - one fuse takes approximately 10 seconds to get completely burnt."

Chaits looked at the length of one fuse & calculated the length approximately - in case he puts the other end on fire, the whole mesh will take about 15 minutes to reach the explosive in centre - he picked up an explosive stick that rested on the top & walked behind Lisha toward the rear exit...

"Do you know has to use a gun?" she asked & Chaits denied, "never mind - use your batons" then she looked at the explosive stick in Chaits' hand "I told you not to touch it - this bloody place is full of arms, ammunition & explosives if this blows up - even the ants won't get any of our leftovers to eat..."

"You forget - I'm the master of poker - I'm planning to use this as a bluff to buy our rescue if it comes to that - don't worry - it is completely safe with me?"

"Ok - c'mon" she urged as they heard banging on the door to the storage room - she opened the rear exit door with caution - a gun cocked in her hand - she expected an ambush - to her surprise - there was nobody there and the door opened to a jetty for the fishing trawlers, to unload their cargo. Nobody was in sight. It was surrounded by sea on all the sides there was no chance for anyone to come around & attack from this side - unless they come over the roof top or on a trawler - they heard the door break off & the guards shouting... Lisha turned around - they heard Cynthia shout instructions – 'she must be raging mad by now!' Chaits gulped saliva at the thought, 'and she'd be seeking Lisha's blood' he looked at Lisha who crouched behind the pier shooting back at them, "Do you know how to swim?" she asked as she changed the magazine of the gun.

"Yes - I do"

"Then - jump and swim away - I'll follow you."

"Not - without you" he said & pushed her off the jetty - heard the splash of her hitting the water & looked at the men who were now running toward him - he looked at Cynthia who was tearing down the jetty at him - he gave her a charming smile & threw a flying kiss at her & lit up the explosive stick & threw at her. The men following her stopped in the middle of the track & ran backward to avoid the blast.

Chaits saw Lisha who was swimming fast toward the shore & followed the suit - he was a powerful swimmer himself & made a lot of ground by the time the stick exploded with a loud bang & ripped away a portion of the jetty - stunning his attackers. It had taken longer than he'd calculated for the fuse to burn - he soon reached the shore & lay panting next to Lisha, to catch his breath ...

"Were you planning a suicide?" Lisha asked.

"No - just planning fireworks for our safety" he said & laughed and she joined him in his laughter as they saw those guards trying to shoot at them & their bullets in the water, ending far away from them.

"C'mon - let's get out of here, we still have a trek to our car & we need to hurry they'll be soon breathing on our back again." she said getting up & heaved Chaits up & they started to trek back to the car - they kept on looking back occasionally to see if the terrorists had managed to think of something & come out to chase them...

"They must be busy closing the doors to the storages" Lisha inferred, "Cynthia must know how dangerous those explosives are... that stock there is enough for a battalion to hold its position for at least 10 days. Now, we can inform police, we now have the proof to nail Wong & his party..."

Chaits looked her "I'm afraid - we don't have the proof" he said "would you like to see some fireworks?"

"I love them..."

"Any moment now" he said & pointed at the warehouse, "by the time you checked the storage vaults - I made a long fuse by tying the box of fuses attaching them to the central vault and lit the fuse - if they haven't noticed the whole place is going to go up..."

"You're dirty rascal" she elbowed him playfully & made a start as they saw cars lining up to chase & hunt for them. The first car was about to start when they saw series of explosions & the sky lit up with its colours - the cars exploded along with - "Adieu" Chaits said as he waived at the inferno & they happily started walking toward the car...

Unknown to them Cynthia walked out - badly battered & bleeding - her eyes threw flames of her hate "You bitch" she screamed in hate, "How did you dare to take him away from me? You'll pay for this - I swear..."

## CHAPTER TWENTY-FOUR

They trekked back to where Lisha had parked her car - it seemed like eternity as they travelled back to the forest house. They were dead tired & slept like logs sure that everyone in that warehouse had been blown away to smoke...

They woke the next morning, their bodies, a bit sore from all the activity - but managed to relax "Good News!" Lisha said as she got up from the computer "our bookings are confirmed for tomorrow - this means – it's bye bye to all the trouble & Malaysia" she hugged Chaits in joy, "this means - tomorrow - we board the cruise to Singapore & in next few days after that - you'll be back in Mumbai & I'll wait for your email confirming my Immigration & our wedding - at my home m Fillipines"

Chaits heaved a sigh of relief finally this was going to be the day when he'd run out of trouble & hugged her back in joy "But" said Lisha, "we still stick to our plan - we take the fishing trawler after midnight tomorrow & board the cruise ın the international waters."

"Why?"

"The way you've blasted the entire warehouse to sky - do you think Wong would let you go peacefully? He'd have sent people, all of his terrorists to seek revenge - just one question Chaits - I want the truth - do you possess that USB they're looking for?"

"No"

"Remember Chaits, we're getting married & trust is something we need..." she searched his face for any give away expression - but his eyes looked directly into hers for a moment & then he said, "I don't have that particular USB with me. I've said this a hundred times that I've thrown away the pouch that belonged to a dead man - I can fight anyone - including the terrorists - but I can't fight a ghost..."

"A ghost?" she looked amused.

"Ya - the way that person's neck was sliced to behead him - I'm certain - he'd turn into a headless ghost."

She looked at him & his serious expression for one long moment & burst out laughing "Excuse me for this - but - do you really believe in ghosts?" she asked amid laughter.

"Not that I've encountered one - but - yes, I've met people who have" he said in self-defence. This made Lisha laugh out all the more. Chaits joined her in laughter glad to deviate from the touchy topic of USB - then he spun yarns about how people had encountered ghosts.

"You should write these stories - I'm sure there'll be takers for these at Hong Kong's film industry." she was awed at the way he'd been describing these encounters.

"In fact that's what I was going to suggest to you... look at you you're beautiful, your face is photogenic, you've a wonderful style when you use your Kung Fu & on top of all this - you're sexy to look at... you'll rule the movies there..."

"What was the last sentence?"

"You'll rule the movies there"

"No - the sentence before that..."

"You're sexy to look at..." and he ran away from her as she charged at him in mock anger - they ran through the house finally she managed a flying tackle as he entered the bedroom - he lay flat on his back, his breath knocked out &

she sat on his stomach wrestling playfully with his arms she slipped & her elbow came down on his chest...

She looked concerned as his eyes shown tremendous pain that flashed - she slowly opened the buttons of his shirt & looked at the swellings around the points where Cynthia had pricked him when she tortured him - she knew at once that if something wasn't done about it, would get worse...

"I think I need your magic medicine" he said in pain.

She looked at it and said, "I don't have a medicine for such deep wounds - but I can use a military technique for this... the one that's used for bullet wounds..."

"What's it?"

"I've some highly concentrated alcohol - that'll take care of you - I hope - you'll be able to bear the pain."

"Well - if that's the only way - I'll bear it."

She smiled at him & brought back a small vial - she dipped in a matchstick & put a drop in the centre of his wound created by the first prick - Chaits had not imagined such a high intensity of pain & screamed at the top of his voice as the liquid flowed in & around the wound - he could bear it no longer even as she finished, tears in her eyes - she couldn't bear to look at him, thus in great pain - he fainted due to the pain & she sat next to him slowly nursing his wounds till they were clear - then she applied another cream to soothe him - he was lost in deep sleep.

'These are the last few moments that I'll get to spend with him she thought, who knows what's in store when we leave tomorrow night - I hope everything goes according to the plan - I won't be sure till we set our foot in Singapore.' She looked at him sleeping soundly and decided to pack the clothes back in their travel bags - she got up & started with her own bag - she saw the oriental dress gifted by Chaits

& touched it to feel the softness she smiled to herself & blushed at the thought - she kept the dress aside & packed the bag - then she packed his bag keeping aside those things he may need - she then put her efforts to prepare an exclusive meal for their dinner...

"Lisha!" she heard his faint voice calling her & rushed to the bedroom - she found him sitting on the bed gently probing the wounds on his chest...

"Yes - honey" she asked in a sweet voice.

"Come here" he beckoned her & took her arms & kissed the back of her arms, "your medication has worked again I feel no pain - at all."

"Wonderful!" she said & hugged him, "perhaps the salt water of sea must have cleaned those wounds when we swam to the shore."

"I believe just one thing" he said, his eyes filled with love for her, "It is Your Love that's worked this wonder."

"Enough of flattery - now, be a good boy & freshen up - you're smelling alcohol..." she pushed him in the bathroom & she entered the other bathroom...

Chaits looked at the contents in his pocket & smiled - it was still there - untouched in his pocket - he freshened up & entered the hall to a delicious aroma & knew that something had been specially cooked for him he looked around but Lisha wasn't to be seen - so he turned the TV on & watched the English news - it was full of the blast at the warehouse. The police were confused at the amount of arms they had recovered from the blasted site & the government had announced a reward to the person who'd give whereabouts of Wong - most of Wong's close aides were arrested or had fled the country or had committed Hara-Kiri. The casino was sealed - this made the place safe for him to make an easy getaway from Malaysia - back to

Mumbai...

Suddenly - he could see nothing - soft hands of Lisha covered his eyes, "Guess what am I wearing?" she asked playfully - he was good at playing this kind of guessing games – Palak Seth, his girlfriend from Ahemadabad had given him enough experience in the fun of guessing it wrong - so he kept on guessing wild dresses & she kept on denying.

"Ok - last chance before I reveal...'

"Oh! Revelations, then I guess you're nude - that's the best way to reveal yourself..."

"Shut up" she said in mock anger as she put a tight slap on his back.

"Ouch!"

She slowly took her hands off his eyes & he slowly opened them. He turned around - she looked absolutely fabulous & majestic - she wore the dress he'd gifted her when he had proposed his plans to marry her - her hair fell gracefully in a thick, shiny gloss - covering a portion of her shoulders near her neck - the long glittering ear rings shown like shiny stars against the blackness of her glossy smooth silky hair - her supple & smooth skin glowed in contrast to the dark colour of the dress. The dress fitted her to a Tee - and showed her curves to an advantage - she was not wearing the long skirt of the dress & the edge of the dress just managed to cover her body till upper thigh with its fluff & fall, showing off amazingly structured & well shaped legs - she looked what Ralph Hodgson had once described – 'Supple & smooth to her slim finger tips' Chaits couldn't stop ogling at her attractive body topped with an amazingly glowing face - he found holding his breath was easy - his heart was stamping inside as if it was on a on a military parade - he licked his dry lips & still found them go dry - her sweet smile melted every emotion that dared to surface - her eyes shone the aura of her love for him as she extended her arms & put them around him like a flowery garland - she gently sat on his lap - and her ripened cherry lips closed on his - they kissed in love for a long time - neither wanting to release the kiss first as they lovingly caressed each other...

"How do you like the surprize?" she asked in voice that was hoarse & husky after the long kiss - she didn't need the answer - his eyes said it all "today is special - same time tomorrow, we leave this place - to our freedom - never to return & to settle down in our married life..." Chaits kissed her cheeks that had turned pink in reply, "Let's make this evening - the most memorable one I know & I want to cherish this - ever..."

Chaits slowly moved his hand feeling the silkiness of her glossy hair & held her in almost a bear-hug in reply... "I'll suggest - let's finish off the dinner formality & then climb up to the terrace to watch the full moon & the romantic effect created by its rays in this jungle..."

"Good Idea!" Chaits agreed & soon they were done with kitchen & they strolled out - hand in hand the other holding the big mugs filled with finest wine they found in the house - they went around to the back where a small iron staircase spiralled into the sky to the roof of the house.

"This way, Chaits" she said climbing the stairs & he followed like a man in dream looking at her as she climbed ahead of him. They reached and stood on the roof. Chaits looked around at the glamour of nature which shone in the bright moonlight - he followed her onto the turf that had been maintained on the roof & sat on the garden chairs that were set in a corner around which lay short stools allowing them to rest their wine mugs. They sat there sipping their wine gently caressing each other's finger tips and looked around at the beauty of the nature around them.

"I'm sad that I'll have to say bye to this lovely country" she said sullen, "but," then she brightened, "I'm glad that I'm going to be with you - Forever..."

"Don't feel so bad about this" Chaits said holding her hand, "maybe, we'll return after 15-20 years - when these terrorists have forgotten everything or may have been killed in encounters - that's quite possible..."

"Chaits!" she said indignantly, "here, I'm trying to forget everything & make this evening romantic - if you don't mind - stop thinking about them for some time..."

"I'm sorry" he said hastily, "I was trying to help by promising that we'll return to a safe Malaysia one day" he turned his tone to a cheerful one as he played with her stiff hand, "Oh! - I almost forgot something..."

"What?"

"I've a special gift for you"

"What's it?" she was excited now...

"Well you've to wait... let you know in some time - I risked my life so that I could get it for you..."

"Oh! Really?" she said, "and when did you get that gift?"

"Just before these terrorists kidnapped me..."

"You mean to say you got out of the car - got the gift & that's when they kidnapped you?"

"Yes"

"You disobeyed a direct order."

"Hold on - Lisha - I'm not a soldier"

"Don't talk to me. You get out of the car - show your face around for them to recognise you - then like mad, I chase you to some desolate warehouse & almost get both of us killed for a gift? You're crazy & I shudder at the thought that I'm going to marry a crazy man like you..."

"Hey! Calm down..."

"Don't talk to me - do you think I'm going to marry you for your gifts? No - sir - you're wrong - I'm going to marry you because - I Love You" she got up from her chair as she spoke & Chaits followed her "You know something - the most precious gift for me is your life - nothing's more precious than that - you'll be punished for this - KNEEL DOWN"

Chaits looked at her furious face & obeyed... "But - I still think that the gift I got for you is precious enough for me to risk my life."

"Shut up!" he held her hand & fished for his gift from his pocket with other hand "Don't touch me I'm very angry" she continued in her fury, "no gift will pacify my anger - you'll have to promise that you'll obey - always..."

"Yes - Madame" he said in serious tone.

"Don't Madame me - and be sure - I'm dead serious - the moment you disobey me - I'll walk off - never to return - now - LEAVE MY HAND - I'm not interested in your gift" she said as Chaits smiled - she didn't make any effort to release her hand that he held "Why do you think that gift is so important?"

"Without it - I can't marry you..."

"Uh?-what's that?" she looked at him curious to know but wanted to show her anger at the same time "I told you - my most precious gift is - YOU & YOUR LIFE..." she looked stunned as Chaits pulled his hand from his pocket & quietly slipped a beautiful diamond ring on her finger - her words stopped before they flowed...

"Darling - allow me - this is your Wedding Ring - now - if I don't get this for you - pray tell me - how would our wedding be complete?" he said smiling at her while still on his knees...

"Oh! Chaits! You're stupid - you are very, very - romantically stupid" she said & hugged him - holding his head against her stomach "But I love this stupid guy "she said, softness returning to her voice as she looked at the beautiful diamond ring & shook her head happily "You idiot - I'd still have married you - even if you had gifted a plastic ring - now get up & kiss me... you're supposed to when you slip a wedding ring up your bride's finger"

Chaits got up & put his arms around her. He looked at her beautiful face that shone in the moonlight & bent on her gently kissing her ...

## CHAPTER TWENTY-FIVE

As the sun set the pace for the next day - they were excited at the prospect of leaving Malaysia & all the troubles there. They drove to Penang & enjoyed a dinner at the Eden Sea Food Village. Kaz Chan treated them to exotic local dishes as his farewell...

"Chaits! I'm going ahead to make the sure that the arrangement is in order - Kaz Chan will drop you near Penang bridge by 1145PM - around mid-night. You'll see a flash light blink - Once-Twice-Thrice & then three times Twice - just like I showed you - just walk toward that light & that'll be my signal to you. If you don't see the light blinking you show the signal - but only once - if you don't see any signal till 1AM - something could be wrong - just run for it & come back to the forest house - I'll join you there - I'm keeping my mobile with you - I'll call you if something's wrong - ok - see you dear..." she kissed him & drove away while he rested in the performer's room - secluded from the crowd, his heart beating faster as the time for the schedule neared...

Chaits hated this long wait which seemed like eternity & kept watching the seconds on the watch - tick by - Lisha's mobile rang out, breaking the silence in the room - he answered the call & froze...

"Hello - Lover boy!" it was Cynthia... with a chirpy voice," your game's over - if you want to see your bitch again - meet me at the Penang Bridge 11:30PM sharp - be sure to be on time, if you don't show up, with every minute that passes - there'll be one needle up her funny arse & every 10 minutes - there'll be a piece of flesh cut off her sexy body & thrown into the water for fish as a treat and yes - be sure that you're alone when you show up or I'll shove a sword up hers..."

"Look Cynthia - I'll be there - but one scratch on her body - I swear I'll rip you apart" Chaits was furious.

"Oh-oh! The lover boy's concerned - Imran - I want him to listen to her sweet voice - Chaits skipped a heartbeat as he heard Lisha scream in pain, "Oh! What a lovely voice - I keep my promise - no scratch on her body till 11:30PM - and she dies if you don't get the USB..." she abruptly cut the call off.

'Oh! Lord! They have kidnapped her now - what should I do?' he sank in the chair furiously thinking his next plan of action. Finally - he decided that enough was enough - he couldn't go on fighting this war single handed - he looked around in his wallet & found Col Khanna's card - he dialled using Lisha's mobile & related his woes & begged for help...

"I'll mobilise all my men & the police force - but that's going to take some time - secondly - I want you to buy time off those terrorists till my men & the police force reaches - you should be able to recognise their flashing lights from far - as soon as you see those lights - do something to grab your girl & get away from there to satety - I don't want you to get caught up in the crossfire - will you be able to do it?"

"I think so - yes - that seems to be the only way out..."

"Good - All The Best" he said in a tone that gave Chaits the confidence, "leave your baggage - with Kaz Chan, I'll get it collected."

"Thank you - Col Khanna" he hung up. He immediately informed Kaz Chan of the danger Lisha was in & told him his plan to rescue her & requested him to hand the baggage over to someone who comes to collect it from the Indian Embassy or the police - he had tough time in dissuading him from accompanying him to the bridge... "Lisha already is in danger - I don't want anybody else to face the danger because of me!"

Chaits took a cab & stopped at the junction where the road forked to the bridge & to the bypass there was a road block for some work that was underway - so the sign displayed. He looked at his watch & cursed - if he walked - he'd be late & he'd seen enough of Cynthia to believe that she'd do exactly the same as she had threatened. He pulled out his roller skates & rushed toward the bridge - he stopped at the end of the bridge & faintly could make out the shadows - there were about 3-4 cars & few people around it - he had not seen any work that was underway & guessed that terrorists must have put those road blocks to prevent intrusion during their operation to recover USB from him - he pulled out the mobile & dialled Col Khanna's number to inform the scene & to know what he had planned...

"Good boy! Now listen to me, carefully - we know the road block has been put up by those terrorists - our team is already positioned around the bridge - as well in the water below to attack them - all you need to do is - get your girl & run away - as fast as you can - my team's watching you all the way - all the best..."

Chaits was now relaxed - his only concern was Lisha's safety - no matter if he loses his life - at least - these terrorists would be nailed... He took a deep breath & skated toward those shadows who watched in glee & triumph of their effort - they finally loomed up as he approached the centre of the bridge - he could faintly recognise Cynthia as she stood in the centre of that crowd...

"Welcome, again, Lover boy" she said in a teasing tone, "so you do love that bitch - hmmm - let's see the USB - you must know how invaluable is the information stored on it - each one of us gets 10K MYR when we get it to Mr Wong - Guys - you ready with your plans to spend all that money?"

"Yes-we are..." was the chorus.

"Another 5K MYR from me to the guy who lays his hands first on the USB - this guy has played it tough for long... it'll still not be an easy task to recover it from him", she turned to Chaits, "Now - Lover boy - may I have it, please?"

He looked around desperately - Lisha was not to be seen "Where's she?"

"She's safe - where's the USB?"

"USB is safe as well - where's she?"

"Look here - Lover boy - this conversation will lead nowhere. You give the USB & you take her with you" Cynthia was now furious at Chaits' counter demand & pulled out her sword, "do you think that it'll be difficult for me to torture you again & get the USB? Why do you want to play it - so difficult?"

Chaits thought wildly - he had to think fast if he had to save his skin along with Lisha's... "Cynthia - do you think that I'll carry a stupid USB with me - especially, when I know you your organization? Also knowing that you have kidnapped her & the USB is her ransom? Think about it - you can torture & kill me and I promise you that you'll get nothing out of me - till I see her - safe & sound - go ahead - TRY ME..."

Cynthia looked at him trying to see if he bluffed but soon realised that he meant what he said - she may have, perhaps, broken his resolve if he was alone & Lisha was safe - but, here was a lover who would go through any level of torture - just to see his love was safe & sound - she looked at her men & waived to one of them - Chaits recognised him - he was the same tough guy Lisha had kicked when they'd walked along the beach of Penang... he watched the big guy move toward one of the cars, he saw another approach Cynthia & whisper something in her ear...

"That's interesting" Cynthia said in a cynical tone, "that's simply interesting - I want you to remove your skates - this guy just related your skating skills..."

Chaits looked beyond her. The big man had opened the boot of the car & had pulled out Lisha. Her hands & feet were tied up & her mouth was gagged - he carried her over his shoulder as if a gunny bag & let her go as soon as he stood in front of Chaits & Cynthia - she fell to ground with a thud & cried out in pain through her gags - then she wriggled around & saw Chaits standing there - her eyes were wide with fear that Cynthia might kill him & tried screaming and shouting through her gags...

"Tch-tch - the wild cat wants to roar - open up her gags - I'd like to know what she wants to say." The big man bent down & opened her gags.

"Why did you come here? - didn't I tell you to run away if I get into danger?" she asked.

Chaits turned to Cynthia "Our deal is she goes off - safely & I hand over the USB to you."

"Oh! No - our deal was - I won't spill her blood till you get here - take her across the road toward the railing & be ready to throw her off at while her limbs are tied - she can drown - unless this Lover boy yields & meets our demand."

The big man pulled Lisha across the road dragging her by hair - she endured the pain without a sound "Make her stand up & let her face me" The big man obeyed - Cynthia then turned to Chaits, "Now - Lover boy - handsome pie - sweety - Gimme the USB or watch her in pain."

"I think I've already told you that I don't know where your USB is & you can torture me - let her go - you've me - torture me away as much as you like - but - let her go - she's got nothing to do with this..."

"I realise my mistake now - last time, we should have kidnapped her instead of you & we could have saved the warehouse with all the explosives we collected - better late than never - THE USB"

"I don't have it."

The big man pushed a knee at Lisha's leg & held her by her hair to stop her from falling.

"The USB..."

"I swear Cynthia - I don't have your USB" The big man punched a powerful blow in Lisha's stomach & she screamed in pain...

"Look here, Lover boy - don't make me angry - well, well, that reminds me of my dart board - I've always used it when I was frustrated - like I am now" Cynthia opened her jacket to reveal several darts that her jacket housed inside & pulled out one - her hand aimed that at Chaits & quickly moved to throw it - Chaits ducked in anticipation but stopped as he heard Lisha scream out in pain again- he looked horrified - Cynthia had thrown the dart across the road at Lisha & he could see it sticking off her shoulder - blood trickling down - before Chaits could say anything Cynthia threw another dart at great speed & an unerring aim at Lisha's other shoulder & she screamed in pain again... "I hope that you are loving this - Lover boy" and threw one more this time aiming it on her thigh & and another one in quick succession at her another thigh" cut her loose - she's now paralysed till those darts are still there I want to see her wriggle around in pain before she dies - she has to know that she can't steal a man from me..." the big man cut her loose.

"Cynthia - please stop it " Chaits cried out in anguish & watched in horror as another couple of darts made their way toward Lisha - this time, the mark was her shins - she buckled up & fell down... "Wait! I'll get you the USB..."

His words were too late as another dart found the mark in Lisha's stomach & Cynthia turned around, "Oh! My! I'm stupid - really stupid - I'd have had this pleasure a couple of days back..."

Chaits knelt down & unstrapped his skates - he stood up with a skate in his hand - he started removing a tape wound around it which seemed to give him the grip when he skated, "That's it – this is enough - I'm mad" he said loudly to himself for everyone to hear it "I'm trying to keep a USB that would fetch every person here 10K MYR - I could've easily negotiated this deal for 500K MYR & got away - RICH - but it's too late. These guys are lucky - they would be in a position to earn that amount" he finished undraping his skate & put a finger in a small niche - lo! He held a USB & he could see greedy eyes around...

"Gimme the USB" Cynthia said in an excited tone & took a step toward Chaits.

Chaits took a step behind & leaned against the railing "Stop! - One step further - and I swear this USB will go over the bridge - into the deep water below - then you can use your fishing trawlers to catch the fish & cut open every fish that you catch in your net to see if it is the correct one who gobbled your USB - I swear..."

She stopped in her track & put her sword back - but now she pulled up a gun & so did others "It's her life against the USB - she'll die & so will you - we'll still get the USB - let her go of while you're still alive & let ME have the USB..."

"No use - Cynthia - your words threaten me no more - you hurt her any more - I drop this USB into the water - bring her here - to me – GENTLY..."

Cynthia desperately thought a counter but couldn't & waived to the big man - who now lifted Lisha gently & walked toward Chaits... "Careful" Chaits threatened - his hand still ready to drop the USB into the water below - the big man gently laid her paralysed body near his feet "BACK OFF" and he backed off and stood behind Cynthia...

"Why did you come here Chaits - you should've left me to die" Lisha asked him in a weak voice...

"Shut up!" he crouched next to her keeping an eye on the terrorists & wiped off a tear as he saw Lisha's plight - he pulled out the dart from her stomach - she let out a huge cry of pain & the blood oozed out of the wound...

"I'm going to die, Chaits - please save yourself" she could only murmur in pain - he pulled out the other darts - one by one to her heart-rending screams - she was now able to move painfully - he had removed the darts that had paralysed her movement - he could see blood oozing out of every wound & gather in a form of a pool... "You lied to me" Lisha murmured in pain, "you've been carrying the USB all this time" she said resting her back against his knee...

"Try to get up - I'll explain once we are free from these bastards" he gave her his free hand which she held & stood next to him "Will you be able to walk?" she tried & she could with lot of pain "Good - try moving your hands & feet to get out of the paralysing effect of those darts" she started moving them & found the movement returning to her body even as she screamed in pain...

"Cynthia - I swear to you now, if I GET OUT OF THIS ALIVE - You Will Pay For All The Pain She's Endured - WITH YOUR BLOOD" Chaits threatened her in his fury "all you want is this silly USB & the 500K odd money that you'll make with this - plus - the lot of innocent people that you'll kill - believe me - you'll never win..." He held up the USB "this USB is worth about 2 million - right? You all will have to earn it..." he turned around & threw it on the road toward the end of the bridge using all his might, "Go - Fetch your 2 million" he shouted & suddenly - there was a scramble - everyone ran toward the USB where Chaits had thrown it...

"Lisha - this is not the USB they want," Chaits whispered, "I bought it at the mall before they kidnapped me."

Lisha put her hand which was now full of blood around him, "You are a dirty bluffer" she said & pecked him, "thanks for saving my life..."

"We are not safe yet - let's cross the bridge" he put his hand around her waist in a tight grip & dragged her toward the other end even as the terrorists searched for the USB - he heard Cynthia's shout faintly & turned around...

"You - bastard - nobody escapes from me" she screamed at them & heard sound of bullets shot at them... one of those bullets brushed Lisha's ribs as she let out a whiff of painful air - she was too weak to run along with him...

"Chaits - I'm hit - please run away & save yourself - let me die" Lisha said pressing her hand firmly on the torn skin near the rib to stop the blood from oozing out...

Chaits looked at Cynthia & other terrorists, they now were shooting at will, the bullets hitting the iron railings around them with deafening clangs - he could also see a company of police approaching them from behind - he lifted Lisha in his arms... "Chaits! Leave me to my fate & go..."

"Not without you" he said & threw her over the railing into the water & jumped in behind her - he could see the dark wall of water approach fast - he saw Lisha hitting water with a splash & braced himself as he hit the water - for a moment he found himself still travelling downward - he managed to turn & started moving upward toward the surface & gasped for breath - he looked wildly around to see where Lisha was - he couldn't see her - he dived into the water again swimming under the surface desperately searching for her. He was totally unaware of fierce gun battle that was on - between the terrorists & the force - his eyes searched only for Lisha - he dived in again and again at various points but there was no sign of her "Lishal!" he shouted in his loudest possible volume in a hope that she'll respond - he was about to dive in again when strong hands grabbed him & pulled him over on a rubber raft...

"Don't worry - we're police" the man introduced.

"Lisha - she's still in the water" he pointed

"We have a search on - don't worry, we'll find her - let me first take you to safety..." he said in broken English & the motor to the rubber raft sped them away to the shore where a medical van greeted them. The doctor injected a calming medicine - his thoughts went blank & he closed his eyes to a deep sleep...

## CHAPTER TWENTY-SIX

Chaits opened his eyes & looked around - the room seemed to be dark & very quiet...

"How are you feeling now?" a gentle hand touched his forehead. Chaits followed the hand & looked at an elderly doctor - by features & accent - he seemed to be an Indian "I'm doctor Swami - I work with the Indian Embassy."

Chaits tried getting up but was weak - the injected dose still had its effect - Dr Swami smiled at him & left - within few minutes - he returned with Col Khanna...

"Good evening, Son" he beamed at him, "I'm glad that you're safe - seems you'd a pretty lousy adventure in this beautiful country - never mind - now that you're here - I'll personally see to it that you reach India - safely. Rest for some time now - your bag & your clothes are in the cabinet over there - change over... we'll talk over the dinner..."

"Where's Lisha?" he asked weakly "The search party is looking for her - I'll let you know when they find her - now rest yourself."

"Drink the soup - it will make you feel better..." the doctor said.

Chaits felt better & energetic as he sipped on "Doctor - it seems that my ankle is hurt - it's paining - is it ok if I tie it up with a bandage?"

"No problems - you can do it - must have been slightly hurt - bandage it tight - if it makes you feel good" Dr Swami advised & left the room - Chaits could smell sea water on his clothes - he opened his bag & searched for a pair of jeans & found it. He took a hot water bath that rejuvenated him & felt ready for action again - all his pain & drowsiness had vanished - he tried opening the door - it was locked from outside - he was a captive there - he tried windows & they too were locked - he sat & looked around - he pulled out the crape bandage doctor had given and firmly tied it to his ankle before pinning it secure... he had a long wait.

About 9PM - the door opened & a security guard escorted him to Col Khanna's cabin... "Welcome, Son, please have a seat - we have visitors who'd like to meet you before we eat our meal."

Chaits sat in front of him - the same chair that he'd occupied when he'd met Col Khanna for the extension of his visa & his extended stay in Malaysia - his hands nervously ran below the table as he expectantly looked at Col Khanna "Have you found her?"

Col Khanna shook his head in denial.

"Please, Sir, please find her - I'm willing to go out there & help the search party - but find her..!"

"I'm sorry Chaits - but you can't leave this place - I got strict orders to detain you here - the police want you for the blast at the Penang warehouse which killed around 500 people who stayed there."

"Sir - they were terrorists - all of them..."

"You know that and I believe you - but for police - few were terrorists - the others were innocent fishermen - so you're the one who's accountable for their death - and if they arrest you - it would mean lifetime imprisonment or execution - further - after you jumped off the bridge - more terrorists joined the fray - many of them died in cross firing - some were caught wounded - while a small band -

supposedly led by a woman managed to escape..."

'Cynthia', he knew at once that she was alive... it must have been her who escaped the police.

"So - you see - your life is still in danger" he continued, "they must be searching for both of you. According to the police reports, Lisha is an innocent guide who got caught up because you hired her services. If they find her - I'm sure - her statement will clear you of charges - we've to wait till she clears your name."

"I understand" he said bending down & adjusting his bandage...

"Is your leg still paining?"

"Ya - this bandage is making it bearable." Unnoticed, he had searched for the chewing gum he had stuck underneath during his last visit...

The intercom rang out loud shattering the silence in the room... "Ok - get them here" Col Khanna looked at Chaits, "We have a couple visiting us they are from Intelligence wing from Special Security in India - they think that you may have some valuable information on the terrorists - give them all the information that you hold."

Chaits nodded and they looked at the door as a couple entered... the man was about in his 40s & the lady was in her fifties - Chaits had imagined a couple of soldiers just like his brother & was disappointed to see old people - his sixth sense told him that something was wrong - he remembered what his brother had said 'TRUST NOBODY TILL YOU MEET ME...'"

They introduced themselves as Ms Madhuri Gupta & Mr Bishnoi. They said that they researched on the trend followed by the terrorists...

Chaits gave them the complete story but - made sure he omitted the every mention of the USB that the Terrorists were after...

"Well - it seems that you're lucky to have escaped from such deadly terrorists" Mr Bishnoi said waiving his head in wonder "I'll recommend a bravery award for you if you can hand over the USB that you possess..."

"Thank you, Sir" Chaits said getting up & walked away from Mr Bishnoi but he followed him & patted his shoulder in appreciation... "In normal circumstances I'd have agreed for the award, but..."

"But what?" Ms Gupta joined in, "you deserve this bravery award."

"I understand your enthusiasm in offering me an award but please understand few things. I don't want any award at the cost of my love - she's missing since our last encounter with the bastards & I've had enough of adventure in trying to save our nation as well lives of millions of innocent people - I'm a normal citizen & not a soldier to keep fighting deadly battles. I don't have any USB with me the one I did possess; I threw it at those terrorists to save our lives..."

"We checked it out - it was a fake one. Where's the original?"

Chaits looked at Col Khanna as he said, "How do you know it was a fake?" and he suddenly grabbed the Bishnoi's arm twisted it behind him even as Col Khanna made his way toward Ms Gupta - she drew a gun - a small gun she had hid in her blouse & pointed at Chaits - Chaits held Bishnoi as a shield between them...

"Stop there in your track, Khanna" she yelled furious that Chaits had seen through them "Chaits that USB contained - nothing. Where's the original one?"

"I told you the truth" he said as he twisted Bishnoi's arm more & Bishnoi let out a scream of pain...

"Your game is over Ms Gupta" Col Khanna said, "You won't be able to leave this premise."

"Don't count on that - I'll kill both of you & scream for help... I can easily put your name as a traitor - now, Chaits - leave Bishnoi's hand & like a good boy tell me where's the original USB..."

Chaits looked at her extended arm pointing the gun at him & mentally calculated the distance between them. He slowly eased off Bishnoi's hand & suddenly pushed him at her. In a reflex - she shot at him killing Bishnoi in the process - Chaits was next to her in a flash & kicked her shin hard - she lost her balance & fell face first - the impact causing the gun to drop off - Chaits instantly kicked it away & Mr Khanna took the charge over even as security guards poured in...

"You're under arrest Ms Gupta - you'll be the one who's going to answer what the USB did contain..." Col Khanna said, "take her into the detention cell..." he turned to Chaits, "We knew that we had rodents in our infrastructure - we didn't know who they were" he continued looking at Chaits "thank you for finding them for us - by the way what's this story about the USB?"

"Well I did see a USB which contained a lot of irrelevant information about various cities around the world."

"Oh! So there is a USB that exists..."

"Existed - I formatted it & threw it at those terrorists - that data's gone - forever."

Next five days - Chaits was a captive & was smuggled out of Malaysia by Col Khanna on special plane - he was sad at the news of Lisha's death. He was thrilled when he met the President & bent down to touch his feet to receive the blessings of the great man...

"It's good that you destroyed their terror plans by formatting the USB" the President said, "however, I understand from the Chief here that if we'd have got hold of their plans - it would've been easier to stop them - because - those terrorists could still manage to get another copy & carry out their plan."

"I had promised my brother that I won't let the information out but, I know - I can trust you. The information on the USB was destroyed but, the information is still with me…" he said sitting on a chair - he lifted a part of his jeans to show a bandage…

"I hope you're ok" the President voiced his concern.

"Don't worry, Sir" Chaits said smiling as he started unfolding the bandage - he then pulled out a small tape that seemingly covered his wound - the President & the Chief of Security looked at Chaits, wondering what he was up to…

Lo! No mark of any wound there - Chaits pulled out a small memory chip of a mobile & handed it over to the President.

"All the information that you need is in that memory card - instead of using it as a memory card for my mobile - I used it as a data card & copied the entire information from that USB into this card before I formatted the USB…"

"That's wonderful" the President was amazed while the Chief avoided his glance - here was a normal citizen, who'd not only saved this information from the terrorists - but, also, had been able to bring it in through the entire security system.

"How did you manage to keep it from those terrorists and other people?" the Chief of Security asked him in wonder.

"I had kept this chip under Col Khanna's desk - stuck to a chewing gum. So - it was never with me. If something would have happened to me - somebody at the embassy would have found it while cleaning..."

He met the security Chief before he left for Mumbai "One small request, Sir - if you ever do capture Cynthia - I'd like to kill her personally."

"I'll promise you that pleasure" he'd said as he watched Chaits depart & shook his head in wonder, 'Hmmm - what a resourceful person - we had sent our operative who failed & was killed despite the training - while this guy made it without any training - I wish, I could hire operatives like him - this time, we discovered him by mistake - probably - we won't commit the same mistake again...'

## CHAPTER TWENTY-SEVEN

*Back to present ...*

The train rumbled into the New Delhi Station & with heavy heart, Chaits alighted - his mind still occupied by fond memories of Lisha. Mechanically, he hired a taxi to the designated hotel & spent the entire day - smiling at each memory of Lisha & then wiping his tears off realising that he'd never meet her again...

By evening, he got over the grief & ventured out. He wandered in the market - he walked around without any specific intention - then he saw an internet cafe' & entered to check his emails - he generally skimmed through all his emails & logged on to the Facebook - he looked at a friend request by someone - absently, he clicked on allow & it opened the account page - he looked at the page & the photo - it was Laila - he read through the information & was glad to know that she now was married to a farmer in Thailand & had realised her dream to settle down in life - he watched the pictures of her wedding & smiled - she seemed very happy...

He strongly evaded his urge to upload Lisha's only photo but couldn't stop from uploading a status... "LISHA - I Miss You..."

He couldn't bear the grief any longer & paid a visit to the Akshardham Temple to pray for Lisha's soul - he walked out of the temple after praying & aimlessly started walking on the road - his train of thoughts stopped as his mobile rang - he looked at the number - it looked like an international call coming in -"Hello" he answered & froze in his tracks...

A sweet voice started singing 'Chiquitita' & his heart started beating fast - "LISHA!!" he cried out in joy - "Oh! My God! Am I happy to hear your voice? Where are you? How are you?"

"Shhh - Chaits" she said happily in a cheerful tone "I can't talk to you forever - so - shut up & listen to what I want to say..."

Chaits shut his mouth expectantly to hear what she wanted to say...

"First of all I want to say - SORRY to you. I'm not what you think. I was always a soldier & had been working undercover to fish out terrorists - then I was assigned the task to protect you - I work for Combined Anti-terrorism Alliance - an organization combined by many countries in the world - this request came up after you spoke to your brother - don't misunderstand me - I had liked you the moment I'd seen you at Eden Seafood village. I was disappointed when an assignment came through. I was actually looking forward to spend a week with you. That's the reason I was in KAL when you reached Penang - I couldn't believe my eyes when they said I'd to protect you..."

"Go on..." Chaits prodded her...

"I was still a soldier when I picked you up from the hotel & left Cynthia fuming - but along the way you melted my heart & turned me into a woman - I never had experienced love in my life - you transformed me from a hard core soldier into a normal girl who started dreaming about settling down in life to marry you..."

Chaits listened to her not quite understanding how to react...

"I'd tendered my resignation so that we could marry & settle down."

"Then why are you still - so far away?"

"Please, don't be angry on me, Chaits" she pleaded, "please try & understand what I say - I was still paralyzed when you threw me in the water from the bridge. I was immediately hauled out & taken to a military hospital - it took over a month for me to recover - I was told that you didn't make it alive & I wept day in, day out - I realised how difficult the life was without you - I was still in the camp - re-training myself to avenge your death - I couldn't get you out of my system..."

"So was I told that you didn't make it alive" Chaits said furiously.

"One day, when I was browsing internet - a thought struck me - I didn't have a photo of you & since, as per the information, you were dead - I wanted - just one photo of you for my memory & as will to fight & demolish all the terrorist outfits. I was surprised to see your profile on the Facebook & was extremely happy to know that you were alive & now into your normal mode - I hate those cute romantic words pasted by your girlfriends there - I approached my commander & demanded an explanation about the news of your death - he asked me to wait for a couple of days and ordered a probe in this matter."

"I can't believe it. Those guys knew that I was alive..." Chaits said.

"Exactly - that's what he told me after a couple of days - the men thought that you were saved by but then you disappeared & the Indian Embassy confirmed that you were missing... That led to belief that it was terrorists who'd captured you may have killed you - and again we debated on my resignation. Then we heard the news of few bombs that exploded in the local trains in Mumbai & I lost the argument - my commander put the ball in my court... 'You can resign & go off to marry him - I'll not stop you - but consider this situation - he could be travelling in one of those trains & the bomb may explode under his seat - everyday - you'll wait in tension till you see him back home - safe & yet be unsure when he goes out again the next day - as against - you be a soldier & kill all those terrorists who would want to plant a bomb that would kill him'. I thought about the options & I chose to be a soldier again - I swore to protect you from all those terrorists who would want to place a bomb to kill you - my love will always remain for you - and my body will be sacrificed to protect you. I follow your posts regularly on the Facebook. I cried again today when I saw your status, you wrote for me - I've taken a special permission to talk to you..."

"I had said and I will say it again - no matter what your decision is - I will still love you... Will I ever be able to see you again?" he asked overwhelmed by her side of the story.

"I don't know - but we'll if Buddha wishes us to meet up again - I LOVE YOU AND WILL KEEP ON LOVING YOU TILL I DIE" Chaits could sense her rears overflowing...

"I'LL KEEP MISSING YOU - LISHA - I keep my word - I respect your decision and will love you... ever..." he said pushing back the tears that wanted to overflow.

"Remember my song - always - when you feel down in dumps" and she started singing 'Chiquitita' again before she cut the call off...

Chaits tried re-dialling her number, but came to a nought as the number didn't exist nor was it recognized by any exchange...

'Was I dreaming?' he asked himself & pinched his arm, 'ouch that hurt - I'm glad - I'm really happy to know that she's alive'. He folded his hands in a prayer to Buddha for sparing her life & begging to meet her again...

At the Combined Anti-terror Cell HQ, New Delhi:

"What's the news?"

"Chief - it seems that Wong has been sighted in Macau - we had been keeping a close watch when one of the casinos there introduced Lucky Charm Girl trend."

"Good, Good! We can nail him down - he should not escape this time."

"But - Chief - we're not yet sure of his exact base. It may take us some time to find that out."

"No worries - better late than never - what's your concern?"

"Bad news... Remember Chaits? His organization is sending him on an incentive trip to Hong Kong & Macau - that will alert Wong..."

The chief bent back on his chair and thought for a while & smiled... "Not a bad idea at all. I think we can use him as a bait to get that bastard out of the hole he's hiding in - last time Chaits got caught up by mistake - this time - it'll be deliberate."

"But Chief - he's not a trained operative."

"That exactly is his plus point - if he was trained - he'd be caught & killed easily - they know how we operate - they can't catch him easily because they can't guess what his next move will be..."

"Chief - that's not fair, dragging in a civilian in this way."

"Everything's Fair in Love & Especially in War."

"In that case - he's going to need a hell lot of protection."

"That can be fixed easily - just let me know what day he is flying to Hong Kong."

"Chief - you very well know that we are still trying to establish our network there - the men we have currently - are unreliable..."

"I know of one person who I can rely on this mission - find out where Lisha is - we will assign his protection to her..."

---------------- xxx ---------------

# Post Word

I had enjoyed writing this book back in 2010. This actually is the second book I wrote. I hope you have enjoyed the story as it unfolded in this book - I didn't have a publisher at that time.

So I had decided to post this story on a blog - https://tchty.blogspot.com...

The cover of this book was designed by my friend Abhijit Pasalkar using AI when we were discussing about it - so a vote of thanks to him for his help. He actually is an entrepreneur and deals with Green Home concept - you can visit his website to see how it could help you... https://microgreenmarvel.com

Thanks for reading this book - I will await your feedback as usual on following links...

Email : pdsspartners@gmail.com

Instagram & Facebook : @pen2me

You can enjoy my other stories ... They are available on Amazon (E-Books included)

- Akhand Hind Fauj - Every Indian should read this story...
- Shadyantra
- The Conducer
- Disposables

**Thank You**